"[Harrison] spares no detail of sex and violence, imbuing every phrase with a visceral punch and a sardonic tone. . . . Truly thrilling."
—*Chicago Tribune*

"Mr. Harrison has produced a thriller that seems to want to be equal parts of Raymond Chandler, William Styron, and Tom Wolfe. . . . These corollary aspirations generate some of the greatest pleasures in Mr. Harrison's novel, so that the same narrative that impresses us with its top-to-bottom knowledge of New York City fauna is also illuminating about the quiet acts of omission that irrevocably damage a marriage."
—*Entertainment Weekly*

"*Manhattan Nocturne* soars."
—*The New York Times Book Review*

3/3

risk

PRAISE FOR COLIN HARRISON

THE FINDER

"A chilling, high-speed roller-coaster of a ride that doubles as a sardonic sightseeing tour of the seamier side of New York City."
—*The New York Times*

"Brilliant ... recalls Tom Wolfe's bestselling *The Bonfire of the Vanities,* but this is a far darker story and a far more interesting one. Harrison's Big Apple is rotten to the core."
—*The Washington Post*

"Brutally effective ... Harrison spins a fast-paced NYC crime novel. . . cancel all other pl ... ent Weekly*

"Harriso... in enough black humor to prove he's more brains than brawn. . . . *The Finder*'s a keeper."
—*USA Today*

THE HAVANA ROOM

"You don't read Colin Harrison; you devour him. . . . It's hard to imagine there will be any books offering more sheer fun than *The Havana Room.*"
—*The Philadelphia Inquirer*

"Harrison is a master of mood and atmosphere, and he gives us in these pages a noirish New York that's at once recognizable as the day-lighted city we all work in, and as frightening as the nightmare place we all dread." —*The New York Times*

"An elegantly crafted thriller you won't want to put down." —*The Washington Post*

AFTERBURN

"Startlingly original . . . A wide-ranging thriller that extends far beyond the typecast confines of the genre." —*GQ*

"Effortlessly weaves together elements of murder, revenge, sexual obsession, obscene wealth, international intrigue . . . Harrison is a master storyteller, whose sure hand switches on the juice beginning on page one and never turns it off." —*New York Post*

"Mr. Harrison is a writer of serious talent. . . . *Afterburn* mesmerizes and convinces." —*The Wall Street Journal*

"*Afterburn* is not just a tightly structured novel of suspense but a rich and textured novel. . . . This is a serious, stylish, generously humane work of fiction." —*Entertainment Weekly*

MANHATTAN NOCTURNE

"A white-knuckle ride . . . With the narrative drive of a hurtling subway express, Harrison plunges readers into a scary subterranean world in which the only comfort comes from the neon flashes of his prose." —*People*

ALSO BY COLIN HARRISON

Rish 2009

The Finder 2008

The Havana Room 2004

Afterburn 2000

Manhattan Nocturne 1996

Bodies Electric 1993

Break and Enter 1990

risk

COLIN HARRISON

Picador

Farrar, Straus and Giroux
New York

RISK. Copyright © 2009 by Colin Harrison. All rights reserved. Printed in the United States of America. For information, address Picador, 175 Fifth Avenue, New York, N.Y. 10010.

www.picadorusa.com

Picador® is a U.S. registered trademark and is used by Farrar, Straus and Giroux under license from Pan Books Limited.

For information on Picador Reading Group Guides, please contact Picador.

E-mail: readinggroupguides@picadorusa.com

Designed by Rich Arnold

ISBN 978-0-312-42893-8

Commissioned by and first published in a different form by *The New York Times Magazine*.

First Picador Edition: October 2009

10   9   8   7   6   5   4   3   2   1

To Ilena Silverman,
colleague, editor, friend

contents

risk

one

AN UNEXPECTED CALL

In my line of work, I've been asked to do a lot of unpleasant things over the years, and I've performed these tasks more or less without complaint. So maybe certain recent events in my life shouldn't have upset me. Shouldn't have knocked me back a step. But they did. Hey, I'm a little older now. The gray is really coming in, though my wife, Carol, says she likes it. In New York City, guys like me end up accumulating dings and bruises and scrapes, just like the banged-up delivery vans you see in Chinatown. Battered, dented, suspensions shot. Engines work but not at high speed. Run, for now. High mileage. That's me, especially these days, after what I found myself asked to do. A strange and unexpected task. Well, I did it but I can't say it was a good thing for anyone, especially me.

I got the call on the second Friday of last April, a sloppy, cold day. The price of oil was bouncing around violently, pushing gold and the dollar in opposite directions with each move. Oil down, dollar up. Oil up, gold up. Dollar down, gold up. The stock market, so recently up after being so recently down, was down again, and everyone I knew was hoping that we wouldn't all be sucked into a giant, cheap-dollared vortex of inflation. Or jolted by yet another sudden drop in economic confidence. Many of the folks in my firm had been slyly loading up on gold for months and no doubt counted themselves smart for betting against the American economy. Me, I'd done nothing slick to prepare for the fiscal apocalypse of the century. All I wanted to do was to go home and have dinner with Carol, maybe sit out on our balcony and drink some cheap wine while we ate. Usually I ask if she's heard from our daughter, Rachel, who was in her first year in college then. Or we gossip about the neighbors, speculating about their sex lives, pill habits, and overall psychic cohesion. Living in an apartment building, you learn things about people, whether you want to or not. Otherwise we'll often go to the movies a few blocks away on Broadway. Or ride the train up to Yankee Stadium, take in a game. Such is the state of our marriage these days. A lot of domestic ritual, laced with middle-aged decay. The occasional half-hearted fight, over the usual topics. Just to clean out the pipes. But neither of us stays angry too long. There's wine to drink, gossip to enjoy. Carol and I usually check in with each other around 4:00 P.M., to see what the evening's plan is, and that was when Anna Hewes called me from the other side of our floor.

"George, I just spoke to Mrs. Corbett."

"The original Mrs. Corbett?"

"Of course," said Anna. "I'm coming over to talk to you."

Mrs. Corbett's late husband, Wilson Corbett, was the founder of our firm, back in the sixties. Anna Hewes was Corbett's old secretary—and I mean old as in "former" but also as in "long past retirement age." Anna spends her time in the personnel office now; they ginned up a job for her when it was clear she was slowing down. But she still arrives early, makes the coffee on her floor, sits in for the receptionist on her breaks, alphabetizes files—that kind of thing. Back in the day she sat in the red-hot center of the universe, when Wilson Corbett was personally running thirty cases at once, sometimes on two phones, working the London bosses, the Chicago investigators, all of them. The guy was a pistol, buckets of energy. He had Anna, and she had two younger women working for her, just trying to keep up.

I'd really liked the guy, admired him. And I owed him a lot. It was Wilson Corbett who'd hired me when I was a kid, pulled me out of the muddy waters of the Queens DA's office back in the eighties. I've been here ever since, too. After Corbett retired, he showed up from time to time, trying to get a whiff of the good old days, but he slipped fast. He'd worked so hard all those long decades that not much was left. Within a few years he didn't recognize people, forgot how to get around the office. His visits dribbled down to just the Christmas party, when he'd shake hands with the people who still remembered him, and then he finally went off and died, as we all do. The whole firm attended the funeral. No one had much discussed Mrs. Corbett, figuring she had plenty of money, a couple of sons—Wall Street guys, as I remembered—and would do whatever old ladies who live on Park Avenue do with themselves at that age.

Now Anna Hewes poked her head in my office. She takes great care with her appearance. Makeup tasteful, dye job perfect, dentures glued in.

"What's Mrs. Corbett want?" I asked.

"She says please tell George Young to come up to her apartment at five o'clock today."

"That was it?"

"If I knew more I'd tell you."

"I'm surprised she even knows my name."

At this Anna gave me a little extra look, but then glanced down, as if she were keeping something to herself. I didn't give it much thought, though; Anna's been at the firm so long that she's gone a little bat-wango. I've learned over the years that 15 percent of the staff is either useless, incompetent, too old, or plain nuts. We get our occasional drunk or heroin addict, too. Anna's been in the 15 percent category for some time now, if you ask me, and frankly, I've wondered why she's still around. But this is the kind of thing the managing partners worry about, not me.

"You have the address?" I finally said.

Anna handed me a piece of paper.

"Five o'clock."

"You have any idea what she wants?"

"She didn't say much, except that her health isn't good."

"She wants me to drop all that I'm doing, prance uptown, and go see her, with no explanation?"

"Yes."

"I'd rather go another time, when it's not totally inconvenient."

"She wants you now, she said."

"I'm very busy shuffling around the fates of desperate people here, Anna."

She gave me a look. She does know the business, I'll give her that.

"It's the right thing to do, George," Anna said. Then she left.

I returned to the work on my desk. I had a lot to do. I always have a lot to do, and generally I get it done in the time there is to do it. The firm is busy, carries about 160 cases at any one moment. Not bad for a small shop. Just a few partners. Plus a handful of career pack mules like me, and the young hotshots who don't stay long once they realize not much changes at the place. Why? Because Patton, Corbett & Strode has a very specialized clientele. One client, actually, a huge, multinational insurance company headquartered in one of the major European capitals. It has a famous old name, but I'm not going to say what it is. Everyone has heard of it, but this company is our client, and we maintain their confidentiality. People hear the company's name and think, What's a few hundred thousand, a million, for a company like that? It's exactly what it sounds like: *money.* We protect their money. Especially these days, when there's so much risk out there.

Our client's business is simple. Some people can't get insurance. Why? They once filed for bankruptcy, they have credit problems, or they own companies in dicey industries. Or maybe they have funny friends. Maybe a criminal record. Or their nationality is a matter of interpretation. They state one thing, the fine print says another. In any case, these people can't get coverage for fire, theft, natural disasters, embezzlement, liability, et cetera. Yet they must have insurance. Must! Somebody insists they have coverage. Who? The bank that so happily wrote them the giant mortgage. Or government regulators. Or business partners. But the applicant can't get insurance through the regular domestic carriers or the mainstream brokers, so they go to high-premium coverage. They pay extra—a lot extra. The previously unnamed company headquartered in a major European capital charges them an enormous premium, all based on the actuarial probability that these customers will, someday after disaster strikes, make a claim. Risk is monetized this way. It can be a very lucrative business. Most people don't realize that the insurance industry has more than two hundred years' worth of data about what human beings do with themselves.

Wilson Corbett himself used to say as much. "People think insurance companies are just mountains of abstractions," he once told me. "But all insurance companies really do is quantify faulty human behavior. They know a very regular percentage of people fall off ladders, crash their cars, and burn down their businesses. They know people are likely to cheat and lie and steal. Can't help themselves from doing it! And one thing correlates with another and that second thing correlates with a third thing, and pretty soon the underwriters know things about individuals before these people even know it about themselves. Sounds impossible, George, but it's true. I've seen underwriters jack up their premiums because they didn't like the tie the guy wore or the kind of car he drove. And they aren't wrong, either. Pretty soon there's a problem."

That's where we come in. When our client receives an American insurance claim it doesn't like, that smells funny, we get involved. I'm not talking petty fender benders or fake slip-and-fall cases. I mean fraud, arson, records destruction. We start asking a lot of questions. How did the warehouse burn down? What exactly was in it? Can you show us the suppliers' receipts to prove the inventory? We always ask for these answers on paper, mailed to us. Why? Because if a claimant lies in his answers and uses the U.S. mail to do so, that's mail fraud. Title 18 of the United States Code, Chapter 63, to be specific. We have special archival files we put envelopes in, so that the ink of postmarks does not fade. So we can use them in court as evidentiary exhibits. When we point out that lying by way of the U.S mail is itself a federal crime, that fact often has a motivating effect on the claimants. So busy were they brilliantly falsifying some other detail that they didn't think of that. The work can be exciting and a little nasty. Which, I confess, is interesting.

This was the business that Wilson Corbett pulled me into all those years ago. I'd soon realized I had to be tough-minded and professionally distrustful. But I liked the work, and it had paid my bills for a very long time now. I owed him a lot, and I try to keep my accounts in order. If Wilson's widow had asked for me, I really did have to go see what she wanted. Plus, if I didn't go, she'd ask someone else in the firm and it might get around to the managing partners that I had turned her down. That was part of my motivation, too, I admit it. Not that it does me any good now, though.

I slipped out at 4:30, not a bad time to get a cab uptown from Rockefeller Center, and by 5:00 was standing in the marble lobby of Mrs. Corbett's apartment building. The tall bellman was a piece of fossilized Irish timber, and his white hair and stiff blue uniform made him look like a retired admiral.

He was hesitant, inspecting me. "Mrs. Corbett, you say?"

I nodded. Maybe this meant she didn't get many visitors.

He dialed. Listened. "Yes, Mrs.— Yes, of course, right away."

The bellman set the phone down, then eyed me. "Now, can you do me a wee favor?"

"What?"

"Keep an eye out for candles. She's been lighting them lately and forgetting. We've had a couple of incidents."

"And if I spot any?"

"Just let me know as you leave. I go up myself to blow them out."

A moment later I rang her bell. The door opened, and a thin, white-haired woman stood there, not smiling, not shaking my hand.

"Mrs. Corbett," I said.

She dropped her eyes down from my face, over my suit and tie and shoes. She'd seen a lot of lawyers in her time, and I suspected they didn't much impress her.

"So you came," she allowed, with no discernible tone of gratitude.

Mrs. Corbett turned and slowly led me back to the living room, a cave of pillows. The place had that sick old-person smell, which was not masked by the candles, their flames flickering. She sat back in an immense sofa.

"Mr. Young, my husband always said you were one of his smartest young fellows, and so I'm depending on him, you see."

"I liked Mr. Corbett a great deal," I told her, glad to say it. "He built the firm."

She settled in, preparing herself. Her ankles were swollen in the way of older people. "I'm going to try to tell you everything," she began. "I'm eighty-one years old. Life isn't exactly what it used to be. It becomes a series of shocks, Mr. Young. Things you never expected." She took a breath, and as she exhaled, she said, "My son Roger died a few months ago."

"I'm sorry to hear that. I don't think the firm got the news."

Mrs. Corbett nodded in a way that meant she preferred not to become emotional. "He was only fifty-one. Divorced, I'm afraid. There had been some business problems. He'd been married about twenty years. I really do like Roger's wife a great deal. Ex-wife, I mean. She's been very good to me, like a daughter. Did you ever meet him?"

"Maybe, if he came to any of the firm parties."

She sighed. "Anyway, Roger was killed in an accident. A plain old stupid accident. I don't want to describe it to you, but all the information is in that big green envelope over there." She pointed to a mahogany table. "He'd just walked out of a bar. He'd been sitting there alone for almost four hours. That much I do know. He wasn't a heavy drinker, absolutely not someone who spent a lot of time in such places."

"Right."

Mrs. Corbett was looking at me intently now. "Mr. Young, the next thing you need to know is that I'm due to have surgery for a very leaky valve in my heart in six weeks. They say that if I don't have the surgery, I'll be dead in about three or four months. Dead as a doornail, my husband used to say. Or if I'm lucky and not actually dead yet, then I might as well be." She smoothed her old hand across a pillow. "So I'm going to do what the doctors tell me. But the operation is almost never done at my age. An old body doesn't take surgery too well. They give me a forty percent chance of surviving."

Bad odds, but she had to take them.

"The operation was only done two times last year in Manhattan on someone my age. One was to that nasty what's-his-name, very rich, trades in his wives every ten years or so. Has that *awful* orange hair. My husband used to play golf with him, said he cheated when he hit the ball in the rough. Well, he lived, unfortunately. The other man, a fine fellow, went kaput on the table."

"So either you die sometime this summer or you have the operation and have a chance to live awhile."

"Maybe even as long as five years. I'll get to see my grandchildren move along. That would be pretty darn good; that would make it all worthwhile, I hope. Now, I called you because I want to know something before I have the operation." She paused, looking at her candles. "I want to know why my son sat in that bar for four hours." Her voice held frustration, even anger, and she twisted the gold bracelet around her wrist. "I want to know what Roger was *doing.*"

"You want to know why he died?"

"No. I know the accident was in fact an accident, but it happened just after he came out of the bar. He was in that bar for a reason."

"You want me to figure this out?"

She nodded.

The city was crawling with retired NYPD detectives trying to pay child support, augment their twenty-years-and-out pensions. "Why not hire someone who—?"

"I did, Mr. Young. He was highly recommended. He got some of the information that's in that green envelope. But he couldn't do it. He said he tried but it couldn't be done."

"I don't know why I—"

"My husband thought you were very capable. Said you were tenacious. I stay in touch with Anna Hewes. I know who's doing what there, you might be surprised to know."

I doubted Anna knew more than what she heard around the coffee machine on her floor, but then again, that might be enough.

"I realize your time is valuable," Mrs. Corbett went on, "and that this might take quite a bit of it, so I'm more than willing to pay whatever you think will be—"

I was already shaking my head. "If I help you I won't accept any money. We can call it repaying an old debt of gratitude to Mr. Corbett, okay?"

She seemed pleased to hear this. I, meanwhile, felt pretty glum.

"That envelope has some other things about Roger. His address, things like that. Some papers and keys."

I had a lot of questions, but Mrs. Corbett eased herself up, overly aware of how much strength it required. She kept one hand on the arm of the chair. With the other she handed me the large green envelope.

"I'll need to think about this for a few days," I said. But we both knew I was going to do it.

In the lobby on my way out, I saw the admiral. "Six candles," I told him. "Five in the living room, one in the hall."

He touched the brim of his blue cap. "Much obliged."

I took a cab across town and along the way called Carol, who was already home, and told her about my visit with Mrs. Corbett. But she didn't sound as if she was listening to me. She did, however, sound out of breath. "What're you doing?" I asked.

"I'm too irritated even to tell you."

Carol works in the compliance division of a huge New York bank that also shall go nameless. You know this bank; it has branches on every other corner. It barely survived the recent fiscal apocalypse of the century by agreeing to swallow one of its insolvent rivals whole, so long as the government gave it the money to do so. Naturally the bank emerged even larger and more omnipotent. As a corporate organism it has cannily weaseled its way into every major global market, buying politicians as necessary in one country after the next, siphoning market share from domestic banks, presenting its culturally customized persona in no fewer than 106 countries. The sovereign wealth funds love this bank and own huge numbers of its shares. Being a naturally suspicious person, Carol has done well at her job. We live on the West Side, with our daughter, lucky to have a nice three-bedroom. We bought in '90, back when the real-estate agents were living on rice and beans. Sometime in the mid-nineties they starting getting fat. Then they exploded. Then they had to live on rice and beans again. The city goes through these cycles, and if you live here long enough you can sense them coming and going. See how the money heats up the city, makes people crazy.

I arrived home, threw my coat on the table. "Yanks and Boston tonight," I called.

"Not good enough," Carol called back. "I want to see Joba."

The Yankees were indeed in Boston that night, with Chien-Ming Wang on the mound. The game would be on television. But that wouldn't cut it for Carol. She wanted to see Joba Chamberlain, the young Yankee fireballer, in person, and preferably from field-level seats.

I'd promised I'd get tickets to the first home game against Boston the coming week. Which I hadn't yet done, perhaps because I was still mourning the loss of Joe Torre as manager, and no amount of happy talk was going to make me feel better anytime soon. You follow a team, you develop these intense relationships. The Yankees still had Mariano, Pettitte, Posada, and Jeter. But they were getting old. And A-Rod turned out to be A-Roid. I'm still getting over that.

I heard the sound of a vacuum cleaner. On for a few moments, then off. I went to the bedroom, where Carol was inspecting our obese cat, which lay belly up, purring.

"What?" I asked.

"Fleas, that's what." Carol frowned at me as if they were my fault.

"You see any?"

"No, but I can *feel* them. I know they're there."

She amuses me, my wife, the bank compliance officer, and she knows it. Which, of course, amuses her. But now she wasn't smiling. "Like this Mrs. Corbett. I've been thinking about it. She's not telling you something, George. Asking you sweetly to do a favor for a little old lady."

"She's a woman in her eighties who's worried about dying, Carol."

"I doubt it's that simple."

"She just lost her son."

This fact didn't much impress Carol. "Why'd she really call you?"

I didn't have an answer.

Mrs. Corbett's green envelope sat on our sideboard while my wife and I ate sushi for dinner.

"Aren't you going to open it?" Carol pointed her chopsticks. "See what's inside?"

In my line of work, investigating and defending against fraudulent insurance claims, you develop a complex psychological relationship with unopened envelopes of all types. Regular paper envelopes, e-mail envelopes, interoffice envelopes with the red tie strings. Before an envelope is opened, you don't know what's in it, and you aren't committed to a course of action. So far as the contents of the envelope go, you're an innocent. The contents may be true, false, incomplete, irrelevant, or stone-cold proof of wrongful intent. But whatever they are, they aren't yet inside your head. They aren't bothering you. They don't affect your sleep, your self-perception, or your faith in the universe. But once the envelope is opened, the contents zap into your brain, where you have to deal with them.

After we finished eating, I opened the green envelope and shook the contents onto my dining room table. Out came a dozen pieces of paper, a smaller envelope, and an unlabeled DVD. There was also a business card of a private investigator named James Hicks.

Carol poked at the papers. "Doesn't look especially promising."

"What were you expecting?"

"Oh, you know, a treasure map, some illicit photographs, maybe a snippet of microfilm."

"This is just a joke to you."

"I know how you felt about Mr. Corbett," she said more softly. "I understand." She lifted up the smaller envelope and drew out two keys on a ring. "I do have one humble request."

"Lay it on me."

"Please do not let this little investigation impinge upon our peaceful, middle-aged existence."

"I won't," I said. "Okay?"

In my battered late forties, I have become, with no apologies to those who claim to know better, a connoisseur of fourteen-dollar bottles of red wine, and now I poured myself a rather large glass and settled in with the effects of Roger Corbett. First I looked at the keys; they looked like regular padlock keys, though of different makes. The envelope they came in also contained a plastic key card for a storage facility downtown. The pieces of paper included a photocopy of Roger Corbett's expired driver's license, which told me that he was six feet tall, 190 pounds (when the license was issued, anyway), with brown eyes and brown hair. I stared at his face; the photo was taken when he was in his late thirties and showed a well-fed white man with a confident glint in his eyes. Strong chin, just like his father, Wilson Corbett. He was wearing a coat and tie. This was the photo of a man on the way up. I remembered his mother saying, "There had been some business problems." So between the time of this photo and his death at age fifty-one, Roger had suffered a reversal. Not so unusual, that; New York City has a way of knocking people around.

There was also a copy of an apartment lease downtown on Broome Street, signed only late the previous year. The monthly rent was $1,700, which, given Manhattan rents, suggested that the place was, shall we say, modest.

There were other papers, but I resisted them for the moment. A hurricane of documentation follows each of us, but what does it really mean? I've got as much paper swirling around me as the next guy, and if you grabbed a fistful of it, you'd learn a lot about my mortgage debt and fatal cholesterol levels and how much world-class fourteen-dollar wine I buy, but not how I worry about our nineteen-year-old daughter, or what I *honestly* think of my wife's hair these days, or how wrong I was about how long my mother would live.

I slipped the DVD into my computer. The color image on the screen showed the outside of the Blue Curtain Lounge on Elizabeth Street, with a time and date stamp reading "1:32

A.M., FEB. 5." The video, shot at perhaps half-second intervals, showed the front exterior of the Blue Curtain Lounge from an unchanging point of view, which suggested it came from a security camera. Taxis flicked by left to right, blurred yellow shapes advancing in jerky jump cuts of time. At last a figure in a dark coat emerged—what appeared to be a middle-aged man pushing his way out the door and then lurching to his left toward the corner of Elizabeth and Prince streets. He looked more or less like the man in Roger Corbett's license photo, plus fifteen years, which is also to say he looked like a million other middle-aged guys. He was not falling-down drunk, not even really loose. He stood at the cross street and seemed thoughtful. Distracted, perhaps. He stepped off the curb, onto Prince, changed his mind, stepped backward onto the curb, pivoted on the ball of his right foot, and, facing the camera, stepped briskly out onto Elizabeth Street as one-way traffic intermittently flowed past. Almost simultaneously he slipped his left hand into his coat pocket and pulled out a small piece of paper that he seemed intent on inspecting—drawing it toward his face, as if to reread and confirm words that he had just read before—when a private carting-service garbage truck hit him full on from his right, carrying him toward Prince and out of the frame of the camera. The piece of paper flew from his hand. I stopped the DVD and went back and watched the garbage truck move left to right across the screen in three jerky frames. It wasn't going any faster than the taxis. Roger Corbett never looked up, not even at the last moment, and I wiggled the file's progress bar back and forth, moving the garbage truck back, to the left, then to the right again, checking. No movement at all, not even his chin lifting, his head turning. Roger was so intent on the piece of paper in his hand that he didn't notice a garbage truck about to hit him at thirty miles an hour.

I sat there. This is what I mean about opening envelopes. Now the unfortunate death of Roger Corbett was embedded in my brain. I know such raw video files are ubiquitous now—the Internet having become an infinite repository of car accidents on Russian highways, small-town convenience-store stickups, high-school brawls, even war executions—but still, it felt weird to be drilling backward in time to the moment that Roger Corbett's life ended. Had Mrs. Corbett seen this? I hoped not.

I started the video again. The rear of the garbage truck disappeared to the right, and then the screen showed traffic slowing, no doubt as the accident became apparent. A man ran from off-screen right, where the garbage truck presumably had stopped, and straight into the Blue Curtain Lounge. A few people stepped out from the bar, noticed the commotion down the street to their left, and wandered toward it, with a provisional curiosity about the fate of Roger Corbett. Indeed, Roger himself did not reappear, but you didn't have to be a brain surgeon to know that the moment he'd glanced at the paper in his hand had been his last.

The screen went dark. I reversed the video back to the point of impact, hoping to see what had happened to the paper Roger Corbett was holding. In that moment it shot out of his hand and was whisked around the near side of the speeding garbage truck, a white fleck of pixels dancing tantalizingly against the blurred green hopper. Then the truck was gone, the paper sucked out of the frame in its wake. For a moment I wondered if I might venture to that corner and poke around in the gutters. But as anyone who has ever legally parked a car on the streets of New York knows, the city is rather obsessive about its street cleaning, and so surely that stretch of Elizabeth Street had been swept a dozen times since. That slip of paper, so fascinating to Roger Corbett that it seemed to have cost him his life, was gone.

two

"THE CZECHOSLOVAKIA LADY"

The next Monday morning I called James Hicks, the private investigator. I noticed that his office's address was downtown on Broadway, near City Hall and the courts. Probably a two- or three-man shop, a couple of old detective buddies who could still get along with each other. When Hicks heard that Mrs. Corbett had given me his name, he let out a long sigh of irritation. "I got better things to do, Mr. Young, than discuss this," he said. "I'd rather be doing something productive, like flossing my teeth, something like that."

"You got ten minutes?"

"She's paying you, I assume."

risk | 21

"No."

He gargled his disgust.

"Ten minutes," I said.

"Where do you work?"

"Rock Center."

I heard typing. Then a pause as he read his screen. "You're a private practice lawyer, specializing in high-risk insurance matters?"

This is the world we live in. They get your name, they get everything. "Yes, that's me," I said.

"Meet me tomorrow morning at the Top of the Rock. Nine A.M., before the tourists get there."

Which I did, arriving in Midtown too early and sitting in a coffee shop making a list of useless questions. I didn't expect much from Hicks, given his hostility on the phone, but I got in the line for the Top of the Rock. It was mostly schoolkids and tourists. Your average New Yorker has never been to the top of Rockefeller Center. Seventy stories up, out in the open air. You look at the MetLife Building, the Chrysler Building. Brooklyn sprawls enormously. I think the view is better there than from the Empire State Building, because you can walk around to the north side and more easily see Central Park, a big green rectangle inside the stone grid. The wind was ferocious on the west side, coming from the direction of New Jersey. I confess I stayed away from the edge of the observation deck because I get a weird trembling feeling in my legs if I stand too close to the brink of anything high. It's been that way since I was a kid.

"Mr. Young," came a voice.

I turned. James Hicks was a tall, gray-haired man. His coat was better than mine. So were his shirt and tie and shoes. His eyes held an unblinking coldness; they had seen more than a man should see in one life.

"Your ten minutes have started."

"Why did you drop the case?" I asked.

"There was nothing there. You've seen the tape by now, right? Guy walks out of a bar, garbage truck comes—boom, and it's say good-bye to Hollywood."

"Mrs. Corbett wanted to know what he was doing that night he died."

"I told her, he was sitting in a bar, the bartender remembered him in a booth, maybe he makes a few calls, then walks out, sort of stumbles around, then whammo."

"You figure out what was on the piece of paper he was looking at?"

"Nope."

"You talk to anyone who knew him?"

Hicks's eyes cut over my left shoulder, then came back to me. "A few people. He was nobody special, some Wall Street guy who couldn't hack it. A rich loser. His wife dumped him and moved with the kids to San Diego to live with her parents. She's pretty hot still, probably has action out there."

"You get into his apartment?"

"Nah. Not worth the trouble. Mrs. Corbett said his place was empty, and I assumed it was rented to someone else, anyway."

"Did he have an arrest or conviction record, anything like that?"

"This guy? No way."

"You run a records search?"

"I didn't need no records search."

I realized I didn't have much time left to ask questions. "Where'd you get the video?"

"I went down there and looked at all the surveillance cameras. This one is from a camera paid for by the owner of the Blue Curtain Lounge. He has it trained on his own building, in case something happens. Didn't even know that the accident was on it."

This information made sense; some of the new insurance policies require video logs of all faces of the building. Harder to burn down your own building if there is 24/7/365 tape on it, everyone coming and going captured on record.

Hicks checked his watch. "Look, here's the deal. Sure, I could find out more about this Roger guy, but then what am I going to tell his mother? The old lady's dying. What's the harm of her going to her deathbed without knowing A, B, and C about her son? Who's it gonna hurt? Answer, nobody."

"What's the stuff you didn't want to tell her?"

"I'm not saying there's anything particular. But there could be." Hicks let this statement dangle in space while he watched my reaction. "My advice? Don't get involved."

"You were a detective?"

"That's what the gold badge said."

"Tours all over?"

"Ended up in Brooklyn, Major Case Squad."

So he'd traveled the innards of the city, seen everything.

"Okay," I began again, "well, did you—"

"Hang on there, champ," Hicks interrupted. "Now I got a question for you. Ready? Here it is. Who are you? I mean really, who *are* you, George Young? Do you know?" He waited for me to answer. When I didn't, he said, "You're some lawyer who pushes around paper in an office, right? The soft butt sits in a nice chair. This isn't something you need to dip into, okay? Not what it looks like, okay? My advice? Don't get involved. Go home and drink a beer, know what I'm saying? We got a little old lady who—"

My cell phone rang. It was my wife.

"George, you still with that investigator?"

"Yes."

"I shot his name into our system, just to see what I might get. Because if he's any kind of problem, he can be connected to me, you know."

As a compliance-enforcement officer, she had to be squeaky clean.

"Get anything back?" I asked. Her bank has a huge share of the city's retail banking market; the chances weren't bad Hicks was a customer.

"A business account. With a lot of cash moving in and out. Might not mean much. Is he being helpful?"

"Decidedly not."

"Let me talk to him."

I held out the phone. "My wife wants to say hello."

Hicks scowled at me but took the phone. I watched his face

sag as she spoke. Then his eyebrows shot up. He started to argue, then thought better of it.

He handed me the phone. "Tough lady you got there."

I knew what Hicks was thinking. *This woman just looked at
my banking records.* He gazed toward the southern tip of Manhattan, the streets and buildings spread out before us. He had
a disgusted look on his face, but it was a complicated disgust; it
contained his loathing for me, but it also seemed to reserve
some contempt for himself, since he didn't have the mustard to
stay with the case. But there was even more to it than that—a
grave awareness of something nasty and unfortunate and rep-
rehensible that he was handing from himself to me, an action
that nonetheless might not provide him much relief.

"All right," Hicks muttered. He pulled an index card from his
breast pocket, holding only the edges, and gave it to me. It had a
name and number written in simple block letters. "You don't
know how you got this number, got that? You want to know
more? Fine, be a hero. This is the place to start. But don't come
back to me. You never saw me, you never talked to me. Got that?
Don't ever call me again." He gave me a hard look, wet-eyed in
the wind, then turned, his long dark coat blown forward, and
took quick strides to get away, leaving me alone and atop the
great and terrible city, fearful of falling, as so many do.

You can find out a lot about a recently dead man on the Internet if you put in some time, even if you are philosophically
opposed to the ease of the endeavor. Let me amend that: you
can find out a lot about a recently dead man on the Internet if
he was part of the world whose existence is recorded there,

however incompletely. Which is also to say if he was part of organized, digitized society, as had been Roger Corbett.

The name on the card that Hicks had given me was Roberto Montoya, but before I called this person and started asking him questions, I wanted to know a little more about Roger himself. I'd seen on the security-camera video how he died. Maybe now I could see how he lived.

So that evening I poured some more of my world-class fourteen-dollar wine and went looking for whatever remains of Roger Corbett were buried on computer servers around the globe. Such a strange time we live in. I like it and I don't. Of course, I found out about Roger in bits and pieces, and some facts suggested an interpretation that was not narrowly provable. But once I put the information in order, I began to get something.

Roger Corbett attended Columbia University, class of 1981, majoring in economics. He immediately got his MBA from Dartmouth's Tuck School of Business, and like a lot of well-credentialed young people in the 1980s, he found his way into one of the cells of the huge money hives in the city, as an "analyst." At the age of thirty-one he married one Valerie Caruth, age twenty-two, whose father owned a large Chrysler dealership in Atlanta. In their wedding announcement, Valerie Caruth was identified as "an actress," but the credits I was able to find involved only several commercials for home-cleaning products, modeling for furniture advertisements, and voice-overs for local radio spots. The earliest photo of her that I could find, taken years later, showed a perky strawberry blonde in her early thirties. It appeared that she had certain charms of contour, shall we say. In an even later photo she had acquired hair the color of Jessica Simpson's. After college (SMU, class of '90), the perky and increasingly blond Valerie Caruth apparently made her way to New York City and met Roger Corbett, who was by then six or seven years into a mid-level Wall Street career and, one might surmise, the owner of more than a few good suits and ties.

But Roger was not a killer, not one of those young partners-to-be at Goldman Sachs or Morgan Stanley. Not top-top drawer. Few are, let us remember. (I myself long ago realized that I was, at best, on my good days, clinging to the underside of the second drawer.) But on Wall Street you can be an inflatable clown and make a lot of money if you are in the right place at the right time, like America in the eighties and nineties. And it appeared that Roger Corbett did make a lot of money, by everyday standards. He and Valerie moved to the Orienta section of Mamaroneck in 1994, to a six-bedroom house on Cove Road that they bought for slightly more than $2 million. Their names appeared on the annual reports for several charitable organizations, and although they were not usually listed as the most generous benefactors, their gifts were midlevel and respectable, as these things go.

Roger and his son, Timothy, appeared in an article about a local youth-league lacrosse team. A color photo showed Roger's brown hair thinning, weight creeping into his stomach and chest and face. The boy, who looked like a good kid, clutched his lacrosse stick enthusiastically. Valerie Corbett's name began to appear as "campaign cochairperson" for several nearby charitable concerns. Roger gave amounts of money to a variety of local and national political candidates, Republicans and Democrats. The sums suggested not congruency of belief but rather an adherence to the expectations of others, perhaps his corporate bosses. His wife's name appeared in a testimonial for a local landscape-design service called Green Acres, in which she was quoted as saying: "We decided the old pool was just too small, and so after the new pool was put in, Green Acres came in and redesigned everything—the formal garden, the pool-deck plantings, and the barbecue area. They performed the job on time and kept the work site tidy. We are totally thrilled with the results."

Roger's career sailed smoothly through the 2000 tech-stock meltdown, but all was not well. He and his wife sold their vacation house on Cooksey Drive in Seal Harbor, Mount Desert Island, Maine, and he changed jobs soon thereafter to another investment bank. You hit forty-five, forty-six in this city, you've got to make sure your feet are on solid ground. Roger lasted two years at the new job, then moved to another firm. His name then appeared as one of eight portfolio managers in a new hedge fund called Goliath Partners Event Dynamics and Global Sector Fund, established in early 2006 and domiciled in the Bahamas. Was this supposed to be the big payday? Many of the hedge funds had been leveraging themselves like mad then, borrowing to buy the mortgage securities that looked so lucrative and that were later revealed to be financial toxic waste. This relationship did not appear to last long, because a year later, Roger was associated with a new Internet venture. Although I'm no expert on hedge funds (who is? Not the guys who run them), I assumed that this meant either that he was thrown overboard or that the fund soon failed. What if he told his colleagues they were taking on too much risk and they dumped him as a doom-and-gloomer? Or maybe it was the other way around.

Anyway, Roger moved on to the Internet venture, which suggested to me that he had put some of his own money into it. His previous job as a hedge-fund manager was not mentioned. The new venture involved the establishment of online real-estate franchises that would provide "personalized and extraordinarily sophisticated" market analysis for potential high-end home buyers. Sounded like pure pixie dust to me, and given what happened to real estate starting in 2007, I doubt it had any chance at all, no matter how brilliant the idea might have been. In any case, the company's site was no longer active, and I assumed it had gone bust.

Meanwhile, the house on Cove Road was sold for $4.4 million, and the wife rematerialized in San Diego as the host of a public-access cable-TV cooking show. Her name was listed on a fund-raiser site for a big local hospital, which had color photos, and I saw she was standing next to a tall, rather athletic-looking heart surgeon of about sixty, as he smiled with sly amusement into the camera, his hand casually wrapped around her waist. I peered even more closely at the photo. The expression on his face translated like this: *I'm pleasuring this woman tonight, and you are not.* The doc looked so good I wondered if he was taking human growth hormone, like some of my older colleagues in the firm, who swear by it, making sure you understand what they mean, heh-heh. Now about forty, Valerie Corbett still possessed her certain charms of contour, and if anything, they had become more charming.

How many children did she and Roger have? Hicks had said there were "kids." And kids cost money. If the Corbetts sold their house for over $4 million, they probably had a few more million in retirement funds and savings. But divorces have a way of burning through huge sums of money. The lawyers, the costs of two households. And maybe they'd borrowed against the value of the house to launch the Internet venture. It was the kind of thing people did so confidently back then, so recently, yet so long ago. That could have eaten up a few million easily.

Where did this leave Roger? Hard to say. His Internet trail had gone dead the previous summer. The last listing was in the white pages, showing an R. Corbett on Broome Street in Lower Manhattan. I checked the map; the address was close to the corner of Orchard. That was it; thereafter Roger had ceased being virtual and existed only in the real world.

I turned off the computer and looked at my notes. The points of information on the Internet suggested a sad and yet not unfamiliar arc. Raised with every economic and educational advantage, Roger Corbett was a young man of middling ability who somehow fell off the happy train of American capitalism. Maybe disorder in the marriage was the cause, or maybe the marriage was a casualty. I could, I realized, find his former wife and ask her a few nosy questions that she would rather not answer.

In the morning I found the index card Hicks had given me and called Roberto Montoya. The phone was picked up, and I heard the sound of machinery, maybe an electric drill. Then it stopped.

"Yeah?"

I identified myself and said I was looking into Roger Corbett's affairs for his family.

"I knew I was gonna get a call like this," Montoya breathed. "Matter of time."

"Any chance we could meet?"

"I'll be at the American Legion park Saturday morning. I got a game at eleven. You want to talk, get there before that."

I asked him where "American Legion" was.

"You ain't from Brooklyn, I guess."

"Nope."

"Take the Belt to Canarsie Pier, straight up on Rockaway Parkway, right on Seaview, one block on your right."

"Thanks," I said.

"Don't thank me," he warned, "I ain't done nothing for you yet, and maybe it's going to stay that way."

Early the next Saturday morning I told Carol I was going for a drive to Brooklyn.

"What? You're going to miss Rachel's call?" Our daughter phoned from college every Saturday morning. It was a ritual we had. Her freshman year had been a little bumpy—boys, tough professors—and the calls had helped her. Her spring exams were coming up, and we wanted to keep tabs on them. Carol shook her head. "You know, George, this whole thing with Roger Corbett, this psychic *expedition,* is really a pain. You're getting a little weird about it."

"I am?"

"Don't you think you are?"

"Yes," I said, "now that you mention it."

"And what might that mean?"

"You tell me, since you seem predisposed to comment."

But she didn't immediately respond, out of anger, which happened to be the emotion I felt as well. "I'm not wasting any more time on this, George, because you're wasting enough for both of us."

It was a good thing I left early, because the pope was in town, screwing up traffic. I cut across to the FDR, whizzed over the Brooklyn Bridge, hopped on the Brooklyn Queens Expressway, then jumped on the Belt Parkway. The Verrazano Bridge soared in front of me, the big red-hulled tankers coming up the river to my right. People who live in Manhattan forget (if they ever knew) how huge Brooklyn is, how you can drive fifteen miles just swinging around the big belly of the borough before you get to Queens.

I pulled into the American Legion fields through a chain-link fence. The gravel lot was jammed with SUV's and minivans, and I saw two umps putting on their uniforms. I walked toward a clubhouse set in the middle of four ball fields. It had been a while since anyone had emptied the trash bins. The fields lay right beneath the flight pattern for JFK, the jumbo jets floating by overhead every minute or so.

The four fields each had two teams warming up, most of the kids black or Latino. I found Roberto Montoya standing at home plate hitting flies to his outfielders. He was muscular through the chest and shoulders, like a lot of baseball coaches, and he swung the bat with a mean, efficient snap. His team was called the East New York Diamond Kings. They wore sharp red and green uniforms and looked like a little professional team, with matching shoes, socks, wristbands, even equipment bags. Montoya saw me standing behind the backstop, hit a few more, then handed the bat to another coach.

"You that guy that called?"

I nodded. He shook my hand without conviction.

"Roger Corbett's family has asked me to look into the situation surrounding his death," I said.

"He got hit by that garbage truck over on Elizabeth Street," Montoya said.

"He did."

Roberto hitched up his baseball pants. "So what's to look into?"

"There were some unresolved matters in his affairs," I said.

His mouth puckered like something tasted bad to him. "What d'you do again?"

"I'm an insurance lawyer."

This seemed to relieve him. "I just thought I'd ask, because you know, sometimes people can get kinda crazy, get all—"

"How'd you know Mr. Corbett?"

"Me? I was his super. I run the building."

Then their connection was a reasonable one. I wondered why Hicks, the private investigator, had been so mysterious about Montoya's identity. "Did you know Roger Corbett?"

"Nah, not really, just 'how you doing,' whatever. He was quiet, no trouble."

"I'm looking for people who knew him pretty well."

"You ask his girlfriend?"

"No, who's that?"

"The Czechoslovakia lady, she lives in the same building."

"What's her name?"

He winced. "Geez, it's hard to remember."

"You're the superintendent of the building she lives in and you don't remember?"

He looked at me. "See, the thing of it is, see, is we play in a wood-bat league here. The city of New York made all the high-school teams go from metal bats to wood because of the safety issue, balls get hit too hard. I like it because the wood-bat game is real baseball. You gotta do all the little things right, got to work the count for walks, got to run out grounders. Everything counts in wood bat, see. Can't fake it no more. But the whole reason they went to metal bats in the first place is that wood bats break. Kids break them constantly. Today my kids'll break one, maybe two bats. A good bat, like a Sam Bat or a Mizuno, they go a hundred bucks retail. Even a crappy bat is gonna cost you fifty bucks. Lotta these kids, see, their families don't got a lot of money, and our organization—"

I pulled out my wallet. "Maybe I can make a little contribution to your ball club."

"That would be very appreciated, let me tell you."

I handed him a hundred dollars.

He lifted his red and green ball cap, looked inside the brim, and fished out a piece of paper. He unfolded it. "Here."

It was a sweat-dampened eight-by-ten color photograph of a woman's hand, posed reaching upward, with a phone number and the name Eliska Sedlacek printed below it. How odd. I studied the photo, a little perplexed.

Montoya smiled at my instant interest. As far as he was concerned, I was getting my money's worth. "See, the thing of it is, when you're a super, people always ask you questions, and you got to be prepared."

He turned and hollered in Spanish at his boys to hustle into the dugout. We were done.

The umps had arrived, and the parents were setting out portable canvas chairs. I would have liked to stay and root for Montoya's team, but I had one Eliska Sedlacek to find, Roger Corbett's girlfriend. I wondered if his lovely widow, now to be seen on the arm of a wealthy San Diego surgeon, knew about her. Maybe. But maybe a lot of things. Eliska Sedlacek. A name that my Internet search hadn't turned up. But why should it have? For better or worse—probably worse—Roger Corbett had left his old life behind before leaving life itself altogether.

three

FIVE SHOTS IN A ROW

In my line of work, we often deal with independent business owners, who are, as a group, driven, confident, smart, and industrious. Rarely do they get into trouble in their twenties and thirties. Not only have they not amassed enough capital and social connectivity to establish businesses of much size, but—and this is more important—they also have not yet been battered around by commerce enough to have cut a few corners. It's the older business owners, in their forties and fifties, who begin to reach for larger prizes. Hooked on leverage, emboldened by past successes, or just plain aware that time is running against them, they start to shave it close. They borrow even more, they shake hands with the wrong strangers, they make sweetheart deals with friends, they get a little sloppy with the paperwork. Also by then they are more likely to be pulling a wagonload of responsibilities: children, spouses, home mortgages, school bills, you name it. They don't want to get into trouble, but a regular percentage of them do, and as their options narrow, they begin to suffer from magical thinking. Their logic goes something like this: *I will do one thing that I absolutely shouldn't do, fool all the right people with my earnest lies, cheat the big nameless corporate entity, and then, having escaped a painful fate, never do it again, I swear—unless I really have to.*

I once spent a week in a motel room in Wheeling, West Virginia, trying to understand how a man who owned a wood-furniture factory could actually burn down the business his father and grandfather had spent sixty years building up. He'd decided that he could not compete against the factories in China and Vietnam that made the same wooden chairs and tables he did, but at one-eleventh the cost. To make the fire creditable, he'd sacrificed all the business archives and mementos of the company, including the rocking chair they had hand-made for President Dwight Eisenhower for his visit to the town. How does a man (and make no mistake, most people who commit high-level insurance fraud are men) decide to do that?

Roger Corbett's business failures, though presumably not caused by such illegality, had the same whiff of quiet desperation about them, and I wondered if he had been working some kind of potentially restorative deal the night he was accidentally killed after walking out of the Blue Curtain Lounge. Why else had he sat in the bar so long? Maybe Eliska Sedlacek knew. I called the number on the flyer Montoya had given me, got no answer, and left a message.

I called the next day, left another message. No call came back.

That night, frustrated that I wasn't getting anywhere, I put on my coat at 11:00 P.M.

"Where're you going?" my wife asked. She was setting out her coffee stuff for the next morning.

"Barhopping." Then I explained.

"You lead a wild life, George Young."

"Oh, please."

"You know anything about bar-and-restaurant book-keeping?"

"No."

"Didn't teach you that in law school?"

I looked at my watch.

"If Roger Corbett paid with a credit card, then the receipt is somewhere in the bar's records. They keep those to check against the paperwork from the credit-card company, to make sure they receive their correct payment. It's important information, as far as they are concerned. If you could get a look at that, it would tell you how much Roger spent that night, whether he was soused or not. Assuming he was alone."

"If he paid cash, then the theory is no good."

"True," she said.

"Then I'd be out of luck."

"You would be, *yes.*"

Carol had a certain look, *her* certain look.

"You suggesting I'd be luckier if I stayed home tonight?"

"Oh, never can tell," she mused. "Luck comes and goes."

True enough, but I needed to leave.

"Please take a cab home," Carol said.

"Not to worry." She was being unusually patient with me, I thought.

"Come home at a decent hour."

"Right."

"And don't drink too much."

Forty minutes later I was downtown. The Blue Curtain Lounge sat on the northwest end of the block on Elizabeth Street, and I stood across from it and found behind me the security camera that had captured the last few seconds of Roger Corbett's life. It was mounted onto the wall about twenty feet above the sidewalk, a hooded electronic eyeball that would now record my entrance into the bar. How dispiriting that we are being captured on camera everywhere we go; the city has tens of thousands of them now, belonging to private citizens, small businesses, large corporations, and of course, the police department. It's a done deal; my own daughter, Rachel, has never known a time when there weren't cameras on her in public.

I inspected the paved intersection of Prince and Elizabeth for signs of the accident ten weeks earlier—an old smear of blood, tire marks, perhaps—and of course there was no indication that anything unusual had ever happened there, that a man's life had been snapped like a stick. Chilling but not surprising. If you live in New York for any time, you constantly confront the indifference of the physical city. Everywhere—every street, block, and building—people have labored, lost, won, lived, and died, and rarely is there any acknowledgment of this struggle. Look at the lighted office buildings; thousands toiling in them every day, lives expiring minute by minute. I'm one of those people, of course, though I prefer not to dwell on this fact.

I pushed through the door of the Blue Curtain Lounge. The place had the perfect degree of sexy, mysterious gloom, and was crowded for a weekday night, everyone looking a good ten years younger than me.

"What'll it be?" said the bartender, who belonged to the shaved-head set.

I ordered a beer and glanced around. If you were going to spend four hours in this noisy place, it'd have to be in one of the comfortable booths jammed with foursomes and fivesomes. The kids looked happy and made me think of my daughter, who no doubt had been to places like this. When you're a parent of a teenager in Manhattan, you find out sooner or later that teenagers have no trouble getting served, especially at some of the Indian restaurants in the East Village, and in Chinatown.

I drank one beer, slowly, then another, taking my time going through a copy of that day's *Daily News*. The pope had gone all out the day before, blessing the gaping World Trade Center site and traveling to Yankee Stadium in the afternoon. Then, as I'd hoped, the bar started to empty out around midnight. People still had to work the next day. The bartender saw me watching people leave. He looked like the kind of guy who might be named Mort.

"So now that you've cased the joint, what d'you think?" he said, putting my next beer in front of me.

"Last time I sat in a bar this long you could still smoke inside."

"Yeah, I thought I'd miss it," Mort said, "but it's better this way. I'll live a few months longer."

I looked at Mort directly. He was glaring at me, mouth tight, arms crossed.

"You want to know why I'm here."

"I know my crowd. You're not part of it."

"About ten weeks ago, a guy sat in here for a few hours, then walked out about one-thirty A.M. and got hit by a garbage truck."

The bartender stared at me. No confirmation, no denial.

"I'm looking into this for his family."

"And?"

"I'm wondering if you were here that night, and anything else I might find out."

"You're not the first one to ask," he allowed.

"You might've spoken to a tall, gray-haired guy named Hicks. Retired detective. Long coat, cold manner. Looks at people with dead eyeballs."

Mort nodded. "He was one of them."

"Them?"

"He was the third one I spoke with."

"Who was the first?"

"A cop, that night. He wanted to know if the dead guy seemed suicidal, or got followed out the door. Had anybody seen what happened, stuff like that."

"Who was the second person to ask?"

"Don't know why I should tell you."

"There may not be a good reason."

Mort appraised this statement. "Go on with your questions."

"His name was—"

"Roger Corbett. Early fifties, a bit of a new regular. Not a heavy drinker. Beer only. This was a Monday night. I was here, yes."

"So far so good."

"He came in with a tall, slender woman. She spoke with an accent. German or Swedish or something. I'm not good with accents, since my hearing's basically shot from working in this place. He spent some time with her, they ate a late dinner, we keep the kitchen open until eleven-thirty, then she left. She's a weird number."

"How so?"

"She wears gloves indoors. Never takes them off."

"That's all?"

"I don't like her, so maybe it's just my problem."

"So she left, then what?"

"Then he sits around and reads the papers, the sports coverage, all that stuff. Killing time, I think, like you tonight. Maybe an hour. Then he makes a call on his cell phone. About one-fifteen. We're starting to clean up. The place is pretty quiet. We turn the music down, try to settle people, get them out the door by two. Most bar fights break out after one A.M., in my experience. So he talks awhile and writes down something on one of our bar napkins. We even discussed it."

"What'd he say?"

"He saw me watching him, and after he hangs up, he says, 'My life keeps getting weirder.' I go, 'What happened?' This job, you talk to people, of course, keep the ball moving. He's like, 'I used to be married and living in the suburbs. Now look at me.' I'm like, 'Did you have a big red lawn tractor?' And he's like, 'Matter of fact I did. Eighteen horsepower. That tells you everything.'"

"Then what?"

"Then he pays his bill—"

"Credit card?" I interrupted, remembering my wife's question.

"No, just a bunch of bills. Lays them down, and—"

"Where was the bar napkin he'd written on?"

"In his hand."

"You see what was on it?"

"Nah."

"Then?"

"Then he pulls on his coat, maybe sticks his hands in his pocket, like you do, you know, sort of make sure everything's in there, keys and cell phone and stuff, and then he walks out and like forty-five seconds later someone runs into the bar saying a man got hit by a garbage truck."

"You go out and see it?"

Mort looked away. He appeared to be deciding something— not whether to answer my question but something more momentous than that. He set two shot glasses out on the bar, poured vodka in both, slid one in my direction, then tossed his back, all of it. I inspected mine, saw him waiting, then followed suit.

"Yes, I did go out and look, and I wish I hadn't." He poured himself another one, and me as well. "I'm not a tough guy, to be perfectly honest, live a quiet life, my son has autism and it's hell on my wife." Mort popped back his drink, let out a little cough. "The job keeps me out of the house, you know? I have enough misery, I don't want to wish it on anyone else. I didn't know what I'd see, and then I saw it, saw this Corbett guy, what was left of him, and it's something you don't want to remember, I don't care how many horror movies you ever saw."

I threw my shot back and figured that was that. I'm a red-wine drinker, after all. But I bet myself that Mort would pour himself one more shot. He smiled sadly, then lifted the bottle again, filled both our glasses. I toasted him, and our glasses clinked.

"Thanks, Mort."

"Who's Mort?" he asked.

"You."

He smiled. "If you say so. Decent name, I guess."

Then we knocked them back. I felt this one in my eyeballs, for some reason.

"Let me tell you two things," Mort said, the vodka audible in his voice now. "Number one, I think that funky girl with the gloves is trouble. Don't know what it is, just my good old bartender's funk-detector."

I liked him now and pulled out my wallet, laid down two

fifties parallel on the bar. "Mort, I'm buying us all these drinks we just drank, you good with that?"

He shook his head. "Nope."

"What?"

"You're overpaying."

He poured us each one more. We knocked them back. I got out a business card and wrote my cell number on it.

"You trying to pick me up?" Mort said, taking the card.

"Just in case."

"You forgot something," he advised.

"I probably did."

"Seriously."

"I remember everything so far, but I guess I am forgetting."

"You're forgetting the other thing I was going to tell you."

"Right. I forgot that."

He poured two more. I didn't want it, but I could see that I had to drink it if he was going to tell me. I knocked it back.

"Good," said Mort. He threw his back, too. "So the other thing was about the second guy, after the cops and before that tall Hicks guy. You asked who this was."

I sort of remembered.

"He was not what we would deem an affable individual. Wide and heavy. A real tomato can. But that wasn't the most important part."

My eyes wanted to sleep for a week or two. "What was?"

"He knew about Miss Gloves, was interested in her, too."

That woke me up. "Why?"

"I don't know. He was the one asking the questions, if you know what I mean." Mort the bartender made a gun with his thumb and forefinger and pointed it at his temple. "So, if I'm you, which I'm clearly not, I'd try to avoid this guy."

Point taken. I pulled on my coat and lurched out the door. And stopped. There, across the street from me, was the security camera, an ugly Cyclops in a metal helmet, all-seeing, yet unknowing. Idiot technology watching me now. A spooky feeling, too, for this same camera had captured Roger's last moments. I raised my fist and shook it at the lens. *You got Roger,* I thought, *but you're not going to get me.*

"What happened?" my wife asked the next morning. I remembered I'd made it home in a cab, but not much more.

"I got drunk with Mort the bartender."

"You snored so loud you sounded like a garbage disposal."

I wondered if this comparison was even possible.

"George, did you really have to go out and get drunk?"

I thought back. "Probably."

Carol was about to leave the apartment, dressed in one of her black wool suits. I can't tell the difference between them. "You find out anything that made all of my subsequent pain and suffering worthwhile?"

It took me a moment, then I remembered. The tomato can, the finger gun to the head. "Yes," I said.

My wife waited expectantly, but I didn't tell her. Nope. It wouldn't be the last thing she'd never know, either.

Eliska Sedlacek finally phoned me at my office the next morning. But I was on a call. It was yet another case of a desperate middle-aged man. Why is America so full of them? The claimant owned a large boatyard and marina in Pensacola, Florida. This location, it may be remembered, was flattened in 2005 by Hurricane Dennis. In this case the insured, a man named Otto Planck, had filed a complete-loss claim for his $2.238 million, eighty-five-foot sailboat, *Becky's Best Boy*, which, he said, he desperately tried to tow out of harm's way and failed, resulting in his rescue in a life raft by the Coast Guard and utter destruction of the boat, which he claimed he saw sink with his own two salt-stung eyes. Our local insurance investigator was disturbed by the condition of a piece of the teak hull of the *Becky's Best Boy* that was found washed up on a local beach. The piece had been broken outward, against the curvature of the hull, seemingly from a great force, and the investigator also noted that Otto Planck had training as a Navy SEAL years earlier. He knew how to blow things up, and he also knew how to survive in extreme weather conditions. The boat, built in 1923 for a minor British industrialist (and no doubt christened with a more stately name), was valuable but would have been tough to resell, given the extensive restoration it needed.

This was not an easy case to pursue, but we got a break when it became known that Otto Planck had just purchased, for $300,000, an eighteen-month option to buy the land adjacent to his marina. Planck was a wealthy man on paper, but the marina was not much better than a breakeven proposition, he was maxed out on debt, and you could rightly wonder where he expected to get the money for the $2 million piece of land. The problem was that the destruction of the asset had occurred at sea, with no other witnesses. We had a time-location record of the storm's intensity, and we could see that the moving footprint of the storm just barely included the location of the presumed sinking. If he sank the boat himself, he sailed it directly into the worst part of the hurricane on purpose. I was about to ask our local maritime claims expert about wave heights necessary to swamp an eighty-five-foot boat when my assistant, Laura, came to my door and said that Eliska Sedlacek was calling again. I told her to put her through.

"Mr. Young, I do not understand why you wish to talk to me."

It took me a moment to switch from a hurricane in Pensacola to my quest on behalf of Roger Corbett's mother. I told Eliska Sedlacek I understood that she'd known Roger Corbett in the last few months of his life and that she'd seen him on the night he was killed. Could I ask her a few questions?

"All right. I talk to you, if it does any good."

She suggested we meet for coffee that afternoon. I knew she'd feel more comfortable if it wasn't too close to where she lived, so I proposed a place on the northwest corner of Broadway and Bleecker. She could walk easily. The restaurant there had sported different names over the years, but its basic attraction had remained constant: big plate windows through which you can watch the world go by. The kind of joint where you sit, eat a piece of pie, and think important thoughts that you later forget.

"How will I recognize you?" I asked.

"I'll be wearing gloves," she said.

I arrived five minutes early and found a table. Eliska Sedlacek arrived ten minutes late, a very tall, slender brunette in her mid-twenties wearing sunglasses and a long red coat. And yes, she was wearing gloves. Everything about her was elongated: legs, torso, arms, and neck. I gave a little wave, and she inspected me for a moment before walking over. Perhaps she found my suit and tie reassuring.

"I am sorry I cannot shake hands. I am hand model and must protect them."

We sat down. I ordered pie and coffee; she requested cranberry juice. I explained that Roger's mother had asked me to find out about him.

"I don't know why I am talking to you since he really didn't like his mother very much," said Eliska Sedlacek.

"Why didn't he like her?"

"He thought she was a liar."

I figured I'd get back to that one. "Did you see him a long time?"

"We see each other nine or ten months."

"So, not so long."

She looked away. Her face was long and bony. Not in any way pretty, plain almost, but for her eyes, a pale blue. She was cautious, distrustful. "It was very intense relationship, for me, one of the most intense I ever have."

I was encouraged by this admission. "Why?"

"Because he was in so much pain. Usually you know with older man and younger woman there is imbalance. He has the money or the power or something." She sipped her cranberry juice tentatively. "But Roger was not interested in that. He was not being the older man, you know what I mean?"

Very often the older man is making payments of one sort or another to the younger woman—unofficially, of course.

"So what was in it for you?"

"That is good question. He was, how you say, a type, an American type. He understood a lot of things about this country that I do not as Czech person. He was a man of the world. You could ask him how does hedge fund work, and he could tell you. How does investment banking work? Why is federal interest rate so important? He knew all these things."

My translation: she smelled money on him, even though he was living in reduced circumstances. "A lot of people know these things, though," I said.

She shrugged. "Also he missed his father, who died maybe about five years ago. He felt he didn't know some things about his father, but his mother, she knew them but wouldn't tell. He had some big arguments with her."

"What was his mood on the night that he died?"

She inhaled and looked upward. "We sat in the bar for a while. We ate dinner. I wanted to come home now because I had to leave for airport very early next morning. But he wanted to wait to make phone call."

"Why did he want to wait in the bar? He could have made the call anywhere."

"The heat in our building was not so good."

"Did he make the call?" There would be a record of that call on his cell phone bill.

"Maybe, I guess so. I don't know. I went home and fell asleep."

"Did you know who he was calling?"

"No."

"When did you find out he had been killed?"

"This was terrible part. In the morning I wake up and he is not in my apartment—"

"You had keys to each other's place?"

"Yes. We are lovers, we are very close. I wake up and he is not in bed with me, and I call him but get no answer, and then I have to go. I have modeling job in London for expensive jewelry and watches. Maybe he is mad at me, I don't know, I think I will call him from airport, which I try to do but no answer, and then I must take my eight-fifty-five A.M. flight to London and of course it is long airplane ride and I cannot call. Finally I call when I get to London but no answer. I was very upset but had this long job, you know, five or six days, and I call and call but no answer, just his message, and then when I come back I find out he is dead."

"What happened to all of his stuff, his papers and bills and things?"

"I don't know."

"But you had a key to his apartment."

"The old wife came, she hired somebody to clean it all out. Nobody ask my opinion. All the books and papers and mail and furniture. The super told me, she come few days later."

"He let her in?"

"What can he do? Roger is dead, somebody has to take responsibility."

"Let's go back to his personal life."

"I knew all about it. He tell me about how messed up is everything. His wife sold the house."

"You ever meet her?"

"No, but I saw her. She was very tan and blond. She came to the funeral with the two childrens."

I'd forgotten about this. "So you went, too?"

"I did."

"Did the ex-wife know you had been his girlfriend?"

"Maybe. She looked at me one time. I sat in back of church. We did not talk."

"Any chance Roger was suicidal? Sort of jumped in front of that big garbage truck?"

"No. He was going through bad times, you know, but I think he was optimist."

"Why?"

"He had some new business ventures going."

"Like what?"

"He didn't say."

"Maybe it was a business call he was waiting to make?"

"I don't know."

"How much money did he have?"

She pondered this question, I could see. Every possible answer reflected on her in some way. "Not too much. I mean, look at the building where he live."

Maybe that meant Roger had no money, or maybe he was just hunkered down. "Well, let me put it this way," I said. "Was this a guy who was worrying where his next hundred bucks was coming from? Or was he worrying where his next hundred thousand was coming from?"

Eliska Sedlacek nodded now. "He had money. I saw his checkbook once, he had forty-eight thousand dollars in his account."

Maybe a lot of money to her, I realized. But for a man who had worked on Wall Street, had once owned a house valued in the millions, it was nothing, dandelion dust. Forced to guess, I'd say that after the divorce he opened a checking account for himself but not a savings account. Whatever he got selling their house and splitting up all the other assets would have been a hefty check that he deposited into the new account.

Back when I worked in the Queens DA's office, they taught us a few filler questions for when you didn't know how to keep the conversation going. I used one now. "What was the most important thing he was thinking about?"

Eliska waved her gloved hands around, and I expected her to say his children. But she didn't.

"He wanted to know who his father was, when he was young. Roger said this was lost time in his father's life, and he never talk about it. He said there were papers he needed but couldn't get."

"Personal papers?"

"I guess."

"He say he was glad his father died before all of this bad things happened to him. But Roger also say he miss his father, and when a parent dies and everything, you know, it stays un-resolved, then the child is never at rest." Eliska looked sad. "This is what I mean when I say relationship was very intense. I learn things about men because he is older than some twenty-five-year-old guy who doesn't know, what is this American ex-pression, diddly something."

"Squat. Doesn't know diddly-squat."

"Right. You understand what I mean about him?"

"I think so."

"You knew Roger, yes?"

"I might have met him, but I did not know him."

She frowned, studying me. "But I feel you know him."

This was a strange moment, and although I had earlier doubted the authenticity of her grief, now I did not.

"I'm sorry, no," I said.

We could have left it there, but something was nagging at me.

"What happened to the key?"

"What key?"

"Your key to his apartment."

"I give it to super." She examined my pie, then forced herself to look away. "I was wondering, do you know what ex-wife did with all of Roger's things from his apartment?"

"No," I said.

"I was just curious because I might have left some things in his apartment."

"Like what?"

"Oh, personal things, you know. No big deal."

I let this statement rest untouched. The ex-wife had cleaned out the apartment rather quickly; had she come across any items suggesting a woman's presence? Maybe, but so what? I wondered about Roger Corbett's cell phone bill.

"What happened to Roger's mail?" I asked. "Where does it go?"

Until this moment, Eliska had appeared to be a composed and at least superficially sophisticated young woman who traveled back and forth from Europe, but my question pierced her self-possession. "I don't know answer," she said quickly. "Maybe you ask super."

"What's his name?" I said, testing her.

"He is— I don't see him so often, I'm not sure."

"What's he look like?"

"I cannot remember too easily."

"But you gave him the key," I said.

"No— I mean, yes, yes, of course."

"Is the apartment rented to someone else now?"

In my younger days, when I was sent out from Patton, Corbett & Strode to depose people—claimants, witnesses, local government officials—I soon learned, in a way I had not fully realized, that people lie. Oh, do they lie, they fib with smiles on their faces, they prevaricate with tears in their eyes, they fabricate looking at you straight on, they perjure themselves with monotone certainty, and they dissemble with righteous indignation. I had edged Eliska Sedlacek onto a ladder of questions where she was now lying with almost every statement she made, and instead of answering my question—was Roger Corbett's apartment now rented?—she appeared to apprehend that she had told so many untruths that they had reached a kind of critical and unsustainable mass, potentially in conflict with one another and, at any rate, increasingly susceptible to discovery and impossible to bear a moment longer. She stood up abruptly and said: "Good-bye, I must go. I can't help you anymore."

She pushed through the door and strode south down Broadway, her hair streaming behind her, eager, it was clear, to get away. I watched her go. Then I realized I had one more bite of pie left. The question, I supposed, was why she had even talked to me in the first place. She had suffered through all of my questions, making up answers as necessary. What was in it for her? People who want something usually end up requesting it. What had she asked for? Anything? Yes. What had she said? *Do you know what ex-wife did with all of Roger's things from his apartment?* Why was this so important to her?

four

ROCKING HORSES
AND COWBOY BOOTS

Two weeks passed. I watched Roger's death on the DVD every couple of nights until Carol told me that it bothered her.

Then Valerie Corbett, Roger's never-not-curvaceous former wife, was suddenly in town, a fact conveyed to me by her ex-mother-in-law, Mrs. Corbett, who called my office and left a message. I called her back and arranged to see Valerie the following Monday. Carol thought this was an interesting development, and hardly an accident.

"We have one dead ex-husband, his sick mother, his Czech girlfriend, and now his ex-wife," she said as we were both getting ready to leave for work.

"The women are obsessing over him," I said.

"That's a pretty typical male analysis," Carol responded. "I think they're obsessing over each other, actually."

"What is a typical male, by the way?" I asked. "Can you describe him?"

"Yes. He's nondescript." She finished off her coffee. "Just remember the poor woman is probably still in a state of shock."

The day was high and bright, and I met Valerie Corbett at lunchtime at the Columbus Circle entrance to Central Park. She didn't appear to be in a state of shock. Not at all. She bounced toward me, looking about forty, tan, and quite fit. With those self-sculpted muscular arms that women her age and station become so proud of. And she wanted you to look at her, to appreciate what it took to keep everything firm and high and tight. Which I did, meanwhile remembering the photo of the silver-haired San Diego surgeon with his hand encircling her waist.

"Mr. Young?"

We sat down on one of the benches inside the park.

"As you know, Diana Corbett has asked me to look into the circumstances surrounding the accident that killed your former husband."

She nodded in a way that made me feel she was governed by grief and determination in equal measure. "I'm trying to just be positive about everything and take care of my kids," she said. "So if this helps Diana, good."

"There's no doubt it was an accident, but Mrs. Corbett

seems fixated on trying to understand what was on his mind before he died."

"Right. Frankly, I want to thank you for sort of humoring her."

Her voice still had a trace of her Georgia childhood in it. "I have a couple of questions," I said.

"Okay."

"I'm trying to get a fix on what happened to your—to Roger's stuff after he died."

She'd been expecting the question, I could see. "Well, we got rid of a lot of our belongings in the divorce. Anything of value went out West in the movers' van. Roger wanted me to have it. I think he thought that if all our stuff stayed together maybe there was a chance for us."

"I take it you sought the divorce?"

She nodded miserably. "So anyway, he moved into this tiny place in Little Italy. I think he kind of *liked* how crummy it was, you know? I was only there once, after he died."

"You moved out his belongings?"

"I paid some movers to box up everything and put it in storage."

"Did you go through all the stuff?"

"Not really. I walked around the apartment, threw out the food in the refrigerator. It was a tiny place. Seeing everything made me feel sad. The clothes smelled like him, which . . ." She didn't complete the thought.

"I understand." I'd cleaned out my own mother's apartment years back, remembered the creepiness of smelling her there.

"The super let me in. I told him I was Roger's ex-wife and I'd take care of everything. I had to pay him a fee to get access. I didn't want to argue about it. Roger didn't have a lot, maybe thirty boxes in all. Clothes, papers, mostly junk."

"How soon after he died did you do this?"

"Just a few days. I was in shock, but I had to get that part of it done with. I was here planning the funeral, going on automatic. We had to call all his old friends and colleagues. Honestly, I was sort of numb. So anyway, I was in the apartment maybe twenty minutes."

"What about his mail?"

She sighed. "We threw whatever was there in a box along with everything else. He wasn't getting much, a few bills. Anything important, like tax stuff, was being sent to his lawyer's office anyway."

"So basically you cleaned the place out, didn't really look through the—"

"I couldn't deal with it. I was, you know, sort of crying the whole time I was there. The movers did everything, taped the boxes, took them down to the truck."

"And what did you do with the storage-unit keys?"

"I left them for his mother. There are three, a key card and two padlock keys. That's the system they use. You need the key card to get from the elevator to the correct floor. I was there maybe ten minutes to see that all the stuff got put into the little room and to sign the papers. I guess all that junk is Diana's, technically, since my divorce from Roger was finished. There's nothing valuable in there, Mr. Young. I don't want any of it."

But her ex-husband's Czech girlfriend wanted something

in that room. I didn't mention this. "I suppose there'd already been a rigorous enumeration and distribution of the marital assets not so long before, at the time of the settlement?"

"If you want to put it that way. He didn't have much money after the divorce."

"Did you tell Diana Corbett where the storage facility was?"

"She has all the paperwork and those keys. Or maybe she gave them to you. There were a lot of details she was thinking about. It was a tough time for her. Still is, of course. I paid for a full year ahead with my credit card, just so no one would have to deal with this right away. If that junk sits there a year because no one wants to bother with it, fine by me. If Diana wants to just throw it all out, that's fine, too. I have all the photos and videotapes from when Roger and I were younger. That's the stuff I care about."

"How's your relationship with Diana Corbett, if I may ask?"

"Basically? Sad."

"Why?"

Valerie opened her hands, as if the answer was obvious. "Well, you know, she's the grandmother of my kids. She's really sick. And my kids just lost their father, and now maybe they'll lose their grandmother."

I suddenly felt rotten about putting her through my questions.

"Why're you doing all this?" she asked, no doubt sensing my lack of conviction.

"Mr. Corbett gave me my job at the firm."

"I see." She studied me closely. But I returned the favor, and noticed how white the sclera of both her eyes were, often a sign of excellent health. We stared at each other, the intimacy a little unnerving, and finally she said, "Roger's father was quite the character."

"He was."

"You ever meet Roger?"

"No. Not that I can remember."

Valerie smiled, embarrassed. "You sort of seem like maybe you knew him a little. Even though he never mentioned you."

Eliska Sedlacek had said something not much different. "No," I finally answered. "So your ex-husband was out late, waiting to make a phone call. Any idea why?"

Valerie shook her head. "I don't know. . . . Roger was trying to find out who he was. He'd lost the path. Drifting. He lost his confidence. We had a terrible time."

"I noticed that he'd switched jobs a few times."

"Yes, at first he thought he was getting into a very good situation. But so did everybody. They all wanted the big money, and I just think the others cut him out. Then he *had* to find a job, any job, and things got a little desperate. I said, Why don't you just go back to what you were doing before? but he said he was too old now, that all these young kids were coming in and getting paid half of what he would have gotten."

I thanked her again.

"Wait, let me ask you one question," Valerie said, "since you asked me so many."

"Okay."

"Did Roger have a girlfriend?"

I nodded. "I think he did."

"You've met her?"

"Yes. She's Czech."

"Right." She shrugged sadly. "Maybe she made him happy."

Another few days passed before I could get to the storage facility, and I had to arrange through Diana Corbett to have my name put on the authorization list. And there were distractions: Carol saying we had to plan our summer vacation; the Yankees swinging cold bats; claimants insisting their losses were legitimate; Carol asking me when we were going to a game; Carol asking what did I think about our daughter taking a mountaineering trip with her college volleyball team; claimants insisting our questions were legally abusive; the Yankees showing signs of life.

Finally I took the subway downtown and walked over to Tenth Street. I'd been expecting the storage facility to have the feel of a painted-over factory, but in fact it possessed the smell and polished surfaces of a new hotel crossed with a minimum-security prison. I had the paperwork and the three keys, and the attendant waved me through without trouble. The elevator key card let me step off on the third floor, and I followed the signs to the storage unit Valerie Corbett had leased.

Along the hallway I passed people adding or subtracting to their stored possessions: unread books, worn and curling shoes, winter coats and cat carriers, problematic bicycles. I passed a space filled with filing cabinets, another loaded with African masks and statues, and yet another stuffed with hundreds of painted canvases. The last one I saw was lined with dressmakers' dummies wearing military uniforms.

I unlocked the padlocks. Inside the door was a well-lighted

space about twelve feet deep, ten feet wide, and eight feet high. Roger Corbett's last effects sat stacked tightly in the middle, and it was apparent that Valerie had rented too much space. But that helped me because I could walk around the stuff easily.

I pulled a Yankees cap out of the pile. A fan, like me! I put on the cap and began poking through Roger's belongings. I was looking for any recent cell phone bills, to find out whom he'd been calling in the months before he'd died, but it was impossible not to sift voyeuristically through all his leavings. I pushed his furniture to one side; it was cheap junk, stained and beaten, bought at least secondhand. The next-largest item was his bag of golf clubs. They were a very expensive mono-grammed set and, of course, a symbol of his better days. I pulled out the driver, gave it a slo-mo swing. Perfect for me. It appeared Roger and I were the same height. The putter also felt perfect in my hands. I dumped out the rest of the clubs to see if anything was in the bottom of the bag, and indeed there was: several pornographic DVDs (all featuring a blond Asian woman with an Islamic moniker), a garage-door opener, and a bottle of mint schnapps. Wreckage from a lonely suburban marriage? I could only wonder.

Onward. I separated the rest of the unit's contents into four categories: papers; books; clothes and personal items; and last, kitchenware and miscellaneous junk. Then I removed a few things I figured belonged to Eliska Sedlacek: a paperback novel written in German, two rather fancy silk bras (size 34B), a long-bristled hairbrush, and a large, clear plastic bag contain-ing a box of latex gloves and a bottle of expensive French skin cream. Should I take these away with me? I didn't like the idea of arriving home with them. I could hear my wife: "Why must you bring some other woman's bras into our apartment?"

She had a point. I set them aside.

Roger Corbett's papers were of most interest, of course, and I sat down on the floor and gave them my full attention. No cell phone bills. But I did find an appointment book that I decided to take with me and examine later, various letters from his lawyer detailing each of his divorce filings (the tone of which suggested that the divorce was more or less amicable, with no impedance by Valerie Corbett's attorneys) and copies of his kids' school reports dated from January. A son and a daughter. I noted that both were doing well in school, receiving A's and B's, perhaps trying hard to get along in their new surroundings. The last item was a receipt for an eBay purchase of a 1975 Manhattan white pages taped to the fat phone book itself. He'd bought it only a week before he died. Expensive, too. Why did he want this? Maybe I could ask Eliska Sedlacek.

The boxes did not look especially interesting, but I poked through them nonetheless. Their contents were mostly books and magazines and shoes, including a pair of almost-new hiking boots I quite admired. I was wearing worn-out running shoes and could not resist pulling them off and slipping my feet into Roger Corbett's boots.

They felt rather good.

I tied the laces and kept going. The rest of the room's contents seemed more or less generic, and I passed over them quickly, with the exception of five heavy boxes of silvery

Christmas ornaments: trains, rocking horses, cowboy boots. These were mixed in by the dozen with little metal toy soldiers about three inches high. The metalwork looked cheap. The boxes held so many of these that I wondered if Roger had been importing them for resale. I held up one of the rocking horses: MADE IN CHINA was stamped on the belly. Somewhere I'd read that the Chinese now dominated the Christmas-ornament industry, whole towns devoted to their manufacture. I slipped a cowboy boot and a rocking horse into my pocket to show my wife. Then I left, with a dead man's hat on my head and his boots on my feet.

On my way home in a taxi, I called Valerie Corbett.

"I have one more question I forgot to ask earlier. When you cleaned out Roger's apartment, were there any cell phone bills in the mail?"

"I can't remember. I just scooped everything up."

"Do you have his old cell number?"

"Yes, of course. Hang on." She put the receiver down. A moment later she returned and gave me the number.

I wrote it down, thanked her, and hung up. Then I called the number, expecting to hear it wasn't in service.

But after five rings, a message began: "This is Roger Corbett. I appreciate your call but am unable to return it at this time. I am eager to speak with you, so please leave me your information. Wit and wisdom also gratefully received."

He had a friendly voice, Roger Corbett did. It even sounded a little familiar to me. But how strange that his cell phone was still working, months after he died. Either the phone company had made a mistake or someone was paying the bill. Why?

"He had boxes of these." I handed my wife the metallic cowboy-boot and rocking-horse Christmas ornaments.

"Boxes?"

"Five, anyway."

Carol inspected the face of the rocking horse. "Sort of ugly."

"Why does a guy with an MBA from Dartmouth have boxes of cruddy Christmas ornaments in his apartment?" I asked. "Of course, there was a lot of other stuff, too."

She pointed at my feet. "Like those shoes?"

"Good, don't you think?"

"You took a dead man's shoes? George, come on!"

"They're great boots. Fit perfectly."

"And you just left your old shoes there?"

"I did, yeah."

Carol shook her head in disgust. I was glad I hadn't dragged home Eliska Sedlacek's lovely silk bras. "This whole thing is starting to affect you," she said. "I'm not joking."

"It's weird, I'll grant you."

Carol studied me a moment, and then her face softened. "You go through his papers?" she asked.

"Yes. Not much."

"You know," she said, "I watched that DVD of Roger getting hit by that truck outside the Blue Curtain Lounge."

"Pretty rough."

"I had one question, though."

"What?"

"If he lived on Broome Street, that was where he was presumably headed after leaving the bar, right?"

"According to his girlfriend, yes. Broome and Orchard streets."

"Then why did he turn left, heading north on Elizabeth when he walked out of the bar?" she asked. "That's the wrong direction. Broome is to the south."

I hadn't thought of this.

"There's really only one explanation," Carol said. "He was starting out uptown. That's the way you'd go if you were going to catch a cab on Houston Street or take the subway to Grand Central."

"Why would Roger be going to Grand Central?"

"He wouldn't be, that's the point. But for a moment he headed there automatically."

I understood. "Because he used to take the suburban train home from there."

"He started in that direction, I think, then remembered he didn't live there anymore."

"He lived downtown."

"He lived downtown in his miserable apartment, he was divorced, he was no longer with his wife and kids, all of it. He'd forgotten just for a moment, poor guy, then he remembered."

"And he turned around and came back and then—"

"Yes," said Carol, her eyes unfocused as she thought about Roger. "It was just a little thing and I wondered about it."

Now and then I am reminded that my wife is smarter than I am. This was one of those times.

five

DENTIST TO THE STARS

Roger Corbett's appointment book for the current year began in the closing weeks of the previous one. He'd blocked out a few days just after Christmas as "kids at Mom's," followed by "kids to LaGuardia." I noticed several appointments with doctors, each preceded by "call Mom to remind." So these were his mother's doctors he was dutifully visiting, with her. I remembered going on these appointments with my own mother years back; not much fun, the medical endgame of the parent-child relationship. December 31 brought a dinner reservation for two at Jean Georges, but nothing more. He hadn't had much to celebrate as the new year arrived.

The margin of each calendar week served also as Roger's personal finance sheet, and I could see that he'd been drawing a thousand dollars a week from his bank account, and after subtracting for rent, food, phone, and other items, was not living particularly high on the hog, especially if he was spending any real time with his Czech girlfriend. Eliska Sedlacek looked to me like the kind of young woman an older man spent money on. Two important days were highlighted, January 28 and March 11, and they involved interviews of some sort, the first at an investment firm in Rockefeller Center not far from where I worked and the next at the Harvard Club. Clearly Roger had been trying to get back on his feet, not easy to do at his age in the shake-shack of the American economy. Of course, the March 11 appointment never took place, for Roger Corbett was dead and buried by then.

Of particular interest to me was a notation every Friday afternoon at 2:00 P.M., an address: 150 Lex. Where did the unemployed, down-on-his-luck Roger Corbett go every Friday? Yoga? Shrink? Acupuncture? Cooking lessons? This was too interesting to ignore.

The next Friday, I chopped a big hole in my schedule and jumped into a cab at 1:30 P.M. It dropped me at the corner of Thirtieth and Lexington. Number 150, on the west side of the avenue, was a place called the Old Print Shop. I pushed inside and plummeted most agreeably back into the nineteenth century—a deep, quiet room with antique prints and maps hanging from the plaster walls, with more maps set on beautiful old wooden display cabinets. A half-dozen patrons browsed reverently, poking through the unframed prints or waiting as a member of the professional staff slid open a flat file. The air itself smelled old, or perhaps this was just the dust of ancient maps rising into the room.

"Pardon me," I asked a man behind the counter, "is it possible that anyone here might remember a man named Roger Corbett?"

"It's not a name I know. Is he a collector?"

"No. He used to come here about this time every week."

"What was the name?"

"Roger Corbett."

"There was a Corbett who made very fine maps of London in the late eighteenth century," he noted somewhat absentmindedly. "But that is not what—"

"I know that name," came a voice behind me. "I know Roger Corbett."

"Ah, Dr. Greenfeld," said the clerk.

I turned to see a small man of about seventy leaning on a cane. He was missing his left arm, and his empty sleeve was pinned against his shirt.

"He sometimes meets me here at this time."

I introduced myself. "I'm afraid I have some unhappy news."

Which I then delivered, in summary form. He said nothing, but blinked several times. Then he let his eyes drift toward the clerk. "You said you had the 1848 Dripps?"

"Of course."

I followed Dr. Greenfeld to the back of the store, where the clerk slid open a wide file drawer and lifted out a large, ornate map of Lower Manhattan dated 1848 that showed, it seemed, the location of nearly every church, meetinghouse, police station, firehouse, ferry route to Brooklyn and New Jersey, and long wooden dock poking out into the Hudson and East rivers. The charting of the city's development barely reached up to Fortieth Street. It was a thing of beauty, at once highly functional in its engraved specificity and yet made mysterious by time, in that it recorded a city long gone.

"Very nice," Greenfeld said. He inspected the price. "Expensive but yes, very nice."

"The condition is good, almost no foxing."

"I could not possibly disagree."

The clerk waited, his sudden silence like a stopwatch being started. Greenfeld handed me his cane as if I were his longtime private valet, extracted a magnifying glass from his pocket, and leaned over the map. He paid special attention to the flattened folds, it seemed. "One minor repair," he noted. "Done well."

"Yes," said the clerk.

Greenfeld straightened. "Please frame it like you did the 1855 Colton, same matte, with the UV glass, too."

"Very well."

He took his cane from me. "Thank you for indulging my weekly passion. I am addicted to maps, and after my wife died, I became nearly unstable in my desire. Now I limit myself to one hour a week in this establishment. You do know where you are, don't you?"

"The Old Print Shop?"

"This is the finest antique map and print store in the Western Hemisphere, my friend. Mecca for map collectors. Oh, there are some other very fine dealers in Manhattan—Richard Arkway, Martayan Lan, Donald Heald, extraordinarily fine, all of them—but I just happen to prefer this place. What else could make an old man feel young but being among things that are much older?"

I didn't have an answer.

"Now you must tell me of Roger."

I explained my role and how I had come across the entries in the appointment book.

Greenfeld took this in, blinking every few seconds as he listened. "We would meet and talk. Informally but with great purpose. You see, I knew his father quite well."

"Roger was on a personal quest to understand him, I think."

Greenfeld nodded. "You're a good detective."

"Well, a lawyer by trade."

"Oh, where?"

I held the door for him as we left the shop. "Patton, Corbett and Strode."

"Ah," said Greenfeld, with greater appreciation. "So you might have known old Wilson Corbett yourself!"

"Yes, but just as a junior lawyer back then."

Greenfeld stole a glance at me. "A dynamo."

We were ambling along under a gray sky, the cane adding a tap to our footsteps.

"You are familiar with Jungian psychoanalytic theory?"

"Not chapter and verse," I said.

"Well, suffice it to say that Wilson was both always himself and never quite who he said he was."

"How do you know?"

"I know, all right. We shared an apartment when he was in law school until the day he was married. I saw a few nice girls in that time. But Wilson, he was quite the magician. Girls appearing and disappearing constantly. Even after he was married to Diana. Into his late thirties. Pathological. Couldn't help himself. Paid dearly for it, too, in all senses of the word."

"How?"

"I don't want to be too specific, out of deference to his memory."

"Of course," I said, feeling disappointed.

"I can say that he broke girls' hearts, he broke his own, he made a few girls pregnant, had to pay to get them out of trouble, which was quite illegal and sometimes dangerous back then, people forget, and I think more than that he did himself great harm. Was haunted by his own youthful promiscuity until a late age, in fact."

"What was your medical specialty?"

Greenfeld grunted. "I was meant to be a psychoanalyst, but I ended up being a dentist for movie and television stars. Yeah, I was big until about 1980, worked on everybody before they appeared on Johnny Carson, Merv Griffin, Mike Douglas. Repairs, bleaching, caps, crowns, you name it, I did it. No root canals, no cavities. I cleaned up all of them, Sinatra, Mailer, Jackie Gleason, Lucille Ball once when she was in town, tried with Liberace, but he took offense, a few times with Karen Carpenter, John Denver, bunch of them, all dead now. Great people. I loved them. Would've kept going, but I lost my arm."

"How, if I may ask?"

"Subway-car door. My own fault. I was saved by a Japanese tourist who used her dress belt as a tourniquet. Wonderful woman. Wouldn't take any credit. I had to call the consulate to track her down and thank her. But after that I was depressed for several years. Because I couldn't work, of course. Not much business for one-armed dentists. Now I see it was the best thing that ever happened to me. Forced me to retire ten years earlier. Now I'm an old man collecting maps."

A lonely old man, too, I sensed. "So what did you tell Roger?"

"I said, Listen, you really want to find this stuff out, you got to talk to other people who knew him. Like Charles Weaver, his father's old poker buddy. He was the true keeper of the secrets, not me. Lives up in Queens, thinks he's the Donald Trump of Floral Park. And Roger did look him up." Greenfeld paused. "Poor guy was lost, searching for ghosts."

"The ex-wife seems to have resettled easily enough."

"Oh, I got the lowdown on *that,* baby. Looks good but a mess underneath. She's got some boyfriend doctor keeping the refrigerator full."

"I thought there was plenty of money, the house went for—"

Greenfeld shook his head. "Roger confessed all that to me. He sank millions into some cockamamie Web site, then millions more into some hedge fund. Maybe it was the other way around. Gone, gone, gone, a marriage, the family"—he looked at me, his voice quieter—"and now the man himself."

In the cab home I watched the buildings go by. It had started to rain, and the wet blurriness of the windows made me feel melancholy. After you've lived in New York for a while, say twenty years, you begin to see the unending conflict between the city that was and the city that will be. Maybe this was why Greenfeld was obsessed with his maps. You walk by a place and what was there is gone. Makes you feel old. The buildings change, go higher, or they get rehabbed and the neighborhood changes. Remember Avenue A and B? Hollowed out, burned out? Squatters in dreadlocks, some of them shooting up in Tompkins Square Park? That's gone, probably for the better. Now it's all million-dollar apartments that no one under forty can afford. Remember the Meatpacking District? Hell's Kitchen? Remember the World Trade Center? Of course. How about Times Square in the seventies? I miss them all, I confess. But my perspective is limited. I'm too young. My mother remembered when they tore down Pennsylvania Station, where Madison Square Garden is now. She used to read about New York, study the history. Canal Street was a canal. Bryant Park was a reservoir. Battery Park is called that because there was a battery of cannons out in the water to protect the harbor. Coney Island was once a real island. The city is always changing, and I find this sad and mystifying.

My mother, I remember, felt this acutely, even though she wasn't a native New Yorker. But she believed that her life began for real when she moved to the city in 1962. She was born and raised in Columbus, Ohio, studied at the University of Wisconsin for three years, was married unhappily at twenty, moved to Milwaukee and worked there as a secretary, and after I came along, divorced at twenty-two. I never knew the guy. Never had the chance. He left my mother and, having nothing better to do, enlisted in the Army and ended up in Vietnam, where he was killed in a forklift accident. His family bitterly blamed my mother for his enlistment and thus his death, and they floated away from her. I never knew them.

Meanwhile, my mother wanted to replant her life; she moved to New York City and almost immediately met a minor UN bureaucrat ten years older named Peter Young who didn't mind that she had a two-year-old son. He married my mother, adopted me as his own, gave us his name, and somehow provided us a decent living on his meager salary. He taught me how to type, throw a curveball, use chopsticks, and shave. He was the best thing that ever happened to us, a good husband and a good father—my real father, as far as I'm concerned. I miss him, every day. I loved him, my mother loved him, and he loved us with all that he had. We were the unexpected bounty in his life, arriving just at the age when he'd given up on having a family after a series of doomed romances. My mother and I knew we were this bounty, and we knew Dad was grateful, because he said as much. He quietly smoked a lot of pot, though, out on the balcony of our apartment, and I think it gave him lung cancer; he died in the mid-eighties, just as I was finishing law school. And about to begin the lost years, trying to be a baby prosecutor in Queens but feeling pretty awful about everything, including how much my mother missed her dead husband.

This was around the time that I got invited to interview at Patton, Corbett & Strode, on the recommendation of someone who had a connection to the firm, and when I got there, Wilson Corbett himself saw me in his office and asked about school and so on. They hired me, and I began my adult life. With my Patton, Corbett & Strode paycheck, I paid off my school loans, purchased my first car, bought my wife's wedding ring; our honeymoon; our apartment; paid the pediatrician's bill for our baby girl, the school bills; the second, third, and fourth cars; the casket for my mother when she died four years ago. I've paid for my whole life as a man with my law-firm paycheck, and I'm grateful. Damned grateful. My life could have been completely different. I could have messed it all up, even before it really began.

As far as Manhattan goes, I know I haven't really amounted to much. I'm not remarkably talented or successful. And that's fine. I'm a guy who lived my life straight, not too many hills or valleys. My wife still can look at me, and our daughter is a good student at a decent university. And it's all because of Old Man Corbett. So the truth of it was that if his widow was calling in an old chit, asking me to find out about her dead son, then I was good for it. I was going to see it through. Come what may. I hadn't said all this to my wife, but I didn't need to. She knew. This was about keeping the big books in order. If Mrs. Corbett died and I'd turned my back on her, then that would be with me forever, and I wouldn't ever be able to fix it. I had enough regrets already, didn't want to add any more.

On the way uptown on Eighth Avenue, the cabbie rapped on the Plexiglas divider.

"What?"

"Hey, pal, you in some kind of trouble?"

"No, why?"

"Somebody been following us since I picked you up. They pulled out soon as we got going."

Both Hicks, the private investigator hired by Mrs. Corbett, and Mort, the bartender at the Blue Curtain Lounge, had told me to watch out for some other people involved with Roger Corbett. "Where are they?"

"Don't look around. Trust me, I seen 'em. White van. You know anybody like that?"

"Nope."

"What d'you want me to do?"

I didn't want anybody following me home. "Cut east on Fiftieth Street!"

I had him drop me on Broadway, where I hopped out after paying the fare. I looked back, and the white van was pulling over sharply. Bad news. The subway stairs are about six steps from the curb, and I zigged through the pedestrians like that new kid who shoots the lane for the Knicks. I moved pretty fast for a slow, old guy, right down into the subway.

I flew through the turnstiles and watched behind me to see if I was being followed. Hard to say. On the platform I hung back to see who was watching me, then jumped on the uptown train just as the doors closed.

Had I gotten away? It seemed so, at the time.

six

THE HAND MODEL'S TALE

Eliska Sedlacek wanted to talk again, and the anxiety in her voice on the phone a few days later suggested that she preferred to do it soon. I told her to meet me that evening at the north end of Union Square and took the R train downtown after work, the guys next to me arguing over the recent acquittal of the three undercover detectives who'd shot a black teenager outside a nightclub. I confess I eavesdropped with only half attention; if you live in New York long enough, these police-killing cases have a kind of sad predictability to them, including the arrival of the politicians into the news coverage, and instead of listening to the men recount what the cops

knew or didn't know before they fired their guns, I preferred
to hope that I would get home early enough to see the last few
innings of the Yankees beating the Tigers at the stadium that
evening.

I came up the steps at Union Square, and Eliska was standing there waiting for me, wearing sunglasses and white gloves
to protect her hands. The gloves added a touch of archaic formality to her appearance. We said hello awkwardly—she kept
her arms at her sides—then found a bench.

"I need to tell you some more things that I did not tell you
before," she began. "It is long story, but it will make sense. Last
night someone call me and say I am in big trouble with them.
They want something. But I do not have it."

"You think I have it?"

"You are only person who maybe can get this thing, yes."

"Okay, lay it on me."

She frowned. "Lay it on top of you?"

"That's an expression. It means fine, tell me what you need
to tell me."

Which she did, at first haltingly, and then with some relief,
never taking off her dark glasses, which eventually meant that I
looked at her lips to understand her emotions. Her English wasn't
so bad, really, and her story was clear enough, if a variant on the
ancient one known as Younger Woman Meets Older Man. The
surprise was that the older man was not Roger Corbett.

Eliska explained that she grew up in a farming village outside of Prague. Her father was adept at fixing the transmis-
sions of broken tractors, and her mother worked in a large
bakery. Eliska played on a girls' high-school basketball team,

and one day while the team was eating in a Prague restaurant after a game, a well-dressed woman came over to her and asked if she could sit down. The woman introduced herself as a talent scout for a Milan modeling agency. She said that Eliska had legs and hands that would be perfect for advertisements that used only those parts. Was she interested? Eliska said she didn't know. Could she still play basketball? No, the woman said, fingers get broken or jammed in basketball all the time. How much did such models make? Eliska asked. When the woman told her, she gasped, knowing how hard her father and mother worked for what little they made. Within a month she was in Milan for her first photo shoot. She was instructed on creaming her hands and keeping them covered. Each night she coated them in cocoa butter and Vaseline, and then she slipped them into disposable latex gloves. She showered with gloves on, rubber bands around each wrist. At age sixteen, she could expect that her legs would be professionally marketable for five years, as long as she didn't gain weight, become pregnant, or have any accidents that scarred her. But her hands could be valuable until she was about thirty, assuming she kept them out of the sun and didn't damage them.

Eliska gave her first few modeling fees to her parents, and they used the money to repair the ceramic tiles of the roof on their house and to buy her father new mechanic's tools. She felt good about helping them, she said, but her new economic status changed things, especially with her mother.

"She feels I look down on her job, that I am too good for her," Eliska remembered. "I think she knew I would not stay at home and that this was sad thing she must get herself ready for. I am just a kid then, I don't understand what is happening, really."

The modeling agency suggested that Eliska move to Paris, which she did, making her parents unhappy. The agency helped her find a flat that she shared with two other young models, a dingy, paint-peeling place near the Gare du Nord, and she soon found that she could make just enough to dress and eat well but no more. The agency seemed to know exactly how much she needed to live on, and the fees appeared to be set so that she had to keep working. And soon it was clear from talking to the other girls that the world of modeling was a brutal class system; she was not in the same league as even the lowest runway models, who were themselves competing frantically for higher pay and visibility. Then there were the famous runway models, ethereal creatures who seemed created out of light and color alone, and looking at them she knew why she was and would forever be known as a "parts" model.

She dated—or whatever it was that young women did with young men. One evening, while she was sitting in a bar with her friends, a portly man in his late thirties introduced himself. He was Russian, and speaking no French or German, he communicated with her in English, which she spoke better than she did Russian. His name was Nikolai Gamov. As a Czech, she was naturally suspicious of Russians, knowing the history of Soviet control of Czechoslovakia, but she found him charming despite herself. She did not mind the age difference; in fact, she liked it. One thing led to another, as it so often does, and soon he was visiting her every time he was in Paris. She came to miss him, and then—yes—to love him. They dreamed that they would move to America someday. He was tired of the danger of being a businessman in Russia, he told her, and felt that under Putin the country was going backward politically. People don't realize, he said, that the price of oil buys Russia its armies. If the price of oil stays high, Putin will take us to war. I saw what happened to my uncles in Afghanistan and to my cousins in Chechnya. In America you do not have to be in the army or navy. When you get an American passport, you can travel and do business in China, South Korea, India, no problem. You are free.

Eliska liked the idea of living in America. And so she and Nikolai planned their future together. She'd move there first and begin the process of becoming an American citizen. Then they'd marry. She sent her portfolio to the New York agencies and was thrilled when they asked her to travel to the United States to do a series of shots that involved modeling an $87,000 watch. Then she was asked to pour wine into a glass. Then model rings. Within a few months she had enough work to get a work visa and rent a cheap apartment at 101st Street and Second Avenue. She flew back and forth to Paris every few weeks— it was a hectic but exciting existence—and Nikolai asked her to take something in her suitcase for him each time. Little toy soldiers. They were heavy and unpainted and did not look to her as if they'd ever been for sale. There were three different ones: a soldier throwing a grenade, his arm cocked backward; another kneeling on one leg and sighting a rifle; and last, a soldier crawling on the ground, one hand holding a rifle. Nikolai sprinkled a few in her checked baggage each trip.

"He tells me put them in a box and he will get them when he comes to America. Sometimes he gives me Christmas ornaments, boots and trains. I fill up one box after next with these things. They say MADE IN CHINA on them, but Nikolai says they are not made in China, they are made in little town outside Moscow with special molds taken from original Chinese ornaments. This is where his family comes from, I know. His brother has business cutting up old cars for parts and also, of course, stealing cars, sometimes from Western Europe, and taking off their identification. I do not ask Nikolai too much. His brother is older, very Russian, heavy and drinks too much. I think he is bad guy. I meet him in Paris when he is with Nikolai. One time I ask, Is these ornaments gold or silver? and he say, No. What is it? It is not something you need to know about, he say. Why am I doing this, then, and he say, For us, for when we live in America. He say, I will tell you some other time, just trust me. He is always trying to get to come to America, he says. Paris is no problem, but he wants to come to America. He has a lot of business, so I say okay, what do I know about this business, especially in Russia, where everything is so much corruption? Besides, also, he treat me very nice, buy me clothes and perfume and everything like that. Sometimes he ask me to fly to Paris just to get his toy soldiers and bring them back here, and most times, I say, Okay, I will do it. Then one time, the last time, last year, he say, You must go for me, please you take very big box of ornaments. I want you to fly from Paris to Montreal and then take train to New York City. They don't search the luggage on the trains. We have a big fight about this, but finally I say okay. So I fly to Montreal and the box comes out to the luggage carousel and I pick it up, so heavy, and then I stay in hotel in Montreal for two days and go to modeling agency there for meeting and then take the train to New York. When you take train into United States, the border agents are very suspicious, but I am ready for them. They ask why am I coming to New York, and I say, I am hand model, first I have meeting in Montreal, then have business in Manhattan, New York. Of course I am wearing my gloves on my hands all the time inside the warm train and this is good proof, you know? Also I have portfolio, very professional photographs. But the agent doesn't like this and the dog comes to smell me and the lady agent takes me to a place and does search on me for drugs. But I have no drugs. They call the agency in Manhattan, and they say, Yes, she is coming here for business. So they put me back on the train. And so I get to New York and take cab to my flat and think I am never going to do this again.

"Then I do my work and after that I try to call Nikolai and he does not answer. I try e-mail, and that is no good, either. Maybe a week goes by, and then I am very nervous. Crying too much, even on job. Then I call my agency in Paris, and they say, Please, you must call someone who left message. It is Russian phone number, and this makes me very nervous so I find a pay phone in bus authority station on Eighth Avenue and wear hat and sunglasses and take off gloves and make myself look fat under a big coat and use phone card that I buy just for this and call the number, and a lady answers and says, We think you should know that they found Nikolai in a hotel room in Pusan. He was tortured and shot dead. They say he stole something from them. I do not know where is Pusan, it is not in Russia. Then she says, There are people who want to talk to you, and I hang up I am so scared. Then I find out Pusan is a city on the coast of South Korea. I think, why is Nikolai in South Korea? Who does he know in South Korea? He never say anythings about that. I know I cannot go back to Paris now, but also everyone who knows me knows where I am living, so I move my apartment in the next few days to Broome Street, all my clothes and things."

"And the boxes of soldiers and trains, that stuff?"

"Yes, all of that I put into four or five boxes. I hired these two boys to move everything for four hundred dollars."

"And the new apartment on Broome Street?" I asked. "That was where you met Roger Corbett?"

"Yes, he lived downstairs from me, and we became friends, you know. I was lonely, and I did not trust anyone, and he was very American and showed me pictures of his family and children, and I knew he was safe. I did not tell him too much about myself. But he was sweet. I liked him. He explained lot of things about how America really work and said he can help me find good lawyer who can get me citizenship papers. I asked Roger could I store some of my things in his apartment, and he said fine. I had the key anyway, you know, because we were seeing each other so much."

"So you moved those boxes into his apartment?"

"Yes, I put them in his closet in the back, and he did not think about them, and I mostly forgot them."

I wasn't sure if I believed that she'd forgotten about them. "Wait, you're telling me that you smuggled these ornaments into the U.S. at the request of your Russian boyfriend. He wouldn't tell you exactly what they were, though it's clear someone had gone to a great deal of trouble to make them. Then your boyfriend was killed because he stole something, you moved because you were scared, and you hid the boxes in Roger's apartment. And you say you 'forgot' about them? Come on."

"Well, okay, of course I am thinking, I know there is somebody in Russia who maybe wants them, but if they find me here they will not find them in my apartment. I am not sure what to do. I do not know who to talk to about them. I don't trust any Russians in this country. And I am thinking, Let me talk to Roger about it, he is so smart, but he has other problems."

"Like what?"

"Like he is finishing divorce, looking for job, all these big things."

All in all, Eliska's story was pretty good; it had money, sex, and violence. I even believed most of it. Whether I believed the right parts was another question.

"Let me see your hands," I said.

She pulled them back. "Why?"

"I'm curious."

"Please don't touch them, though."

"Not to worry."

Turning toward me on the park bench, she loosened the fingertips on one glove and then the other. She checked to be sure I understood that this was a great intimacy for her, that her hands were not just protected but a forbidden sight, especially outside in the fading summer evening. She pulled the gloves off and raised her hands aloft in professional display. They were beautiful and pale, the fingers surprisingly long. And of course, they matched the rest of her—her long neck and arms, torso and legs. She rotated her hands in space, as if each held an invisible fruit.

These were ethereal fingers that touched only luxuries: diamonds, gold, watches, the smooth skin of cars that cost more than houses. Her nails were clean and perfect. These were hands that no longer grabbed or pinched or scratched; they suggested immortality and perfection. Having seen them without gloves— naked, even—I understood why she kept them covered.

"Did Nikolai like your hands?" I found myself asking.

"Of course," she said, "but—"

"But what?"

"But he did not see them very often." Eliska paused, smiled to herself. "Only on special occasions."

And with that, perhaps knowing she could change the mood of the conversation, she reached out her right hand and brushed her long fingers ever so softly along my face, down my cheek, and then beguilingly across my lips. "You see how soft they are."

I did, and in that moment I closed my eyes and suddenly knew Roger. These were the fingers that had touched him, given him solace.

Eliska saw my response. "So maybe you help me?" she asked.

That night I watched Detroit beat the Yankees for the second night in a row. The team wasn't hitting in the clutch. Only Jeter was consistent. And the middle relievers looked shaky. Like a lot of Yankee fans, I find my mood fluctuates with the fate of the team. And my mood was sour.

Then again, perhaps I was just trying to avoid thinking about Eliska Sedlacek and her exotically soft hand trailing down my middle-aged cheek. As she'd expected, her silky fingers had sent excited signals down the subway track to distant stations. But this wasn't all that had gotten me worked up, no sir.

My wife reads in bed most nights, usually this month's thriller of the decade, and after she'd happily tucked in, I slipped into my home office and got onto the Internet. I knew that *Pravda*, the Russian newspaper, maintained an English-language Web site, and I not so casually typed in Nikolai Gamov's name. He seemed worth a Google, anyway—and, oh, boy, a story appeared, condensed from one originally published in the *Seoul Herald*. It explained that Gamov had been shot eight times and that a gun recovered at the scene was identified as "a Baikal," a make manufactured in Russia. Gamov, the article noted, had been "suspected of illegal trading practices."

I sat back in my chair, a little shocked. The girlfriend of a murdered Russian mobster wanted *me* to retrieve boxes of items he'd smuggled into America. Should I do it? Maybe not. Was I in real trouble? Maybe yes. I had to assume that whoever the miscreants were who killed Gamov knew about the smuggled items, in which case they might know about Eliska and might even know about me, too. Was this who had followed my taxi?

Think, George, I told myself. *How can you help yourself, how can you dance away from possible ensnarement?* I had an old school friend named Anthony G. who had dealt with matters like this. I could ask him. But it could take a while to reach Anthony. Meanwhile, I remembered Eliska claimed that Roger Corbett had no idea what was in the boxes she'd put in his apartment. Maybe this was true, maybe not. Either way, my investigation now took on added urgency. Did he know about Nikolai Gamov? Did he know that his new girlfriend had smuggled items and hidden them in his own apartment? Was Roger's last call related to this arrangement? And how about the piece of paper Roger was studying the moment he died? Could Gamov's name have been on it?

The question, I realized, then became who else had been talking with Roger in the last weeks of his life. I recalled that Dr. Greenfeld, the retired dentist to the stars whom I'd met in the print shop, had referred to a Charles Weaver in Queens as "the keeper of the secrets" of Roger's father, and that Roger had tracked him down.

Which, the next morning I did also, without much trouble, using my firm's online access to city real-estate records. I found an address for a dry cleaner in Floral Park and called. A voice answered, grumpy as hell but pleased to be grumpy, too. I explained why I was calling, not that he much cared. He sounded about eighty. One of those old guys who still has mustard on his hot dog. "You wanna talk to me, fine, I'll be playing poker," croaked Charles Weaver. "Just don't expect nothing, okay?"

seven

CASH OR CHECK?

I drove out to Floral Park, taking the Long Island Expressway to the Cross Island Parkway, got off, and soon I was nosing along Jamaica Avenue, looking for Weaver's dry-cleaning shop and listening to the Yankees playing Cleveland at home, Pettitte pitching well.

I found the place, parked, heard Jeter take a fastball, turned off the car, and went inside. A tired old man was also listening to the game, and we followed the rest of the at bat together.

"What can I do for you?"

"I'm George Young. We spoke earlier."

He inspected my suit. "No, we didn't."

"You Charles Weaver?"

"I'm his much more handsome brother. He's in the back."

I followed the man through the narrow passageway, my shoulders brushing skirts and dress pants sheathed in clear bags, and he pushed through to a dank room with four old men playing cards. None had much hair. They'd set out a table with beer, pickles in a bowl, and what looked like fried-fish sandwiches.

"Charlie, guy says he called you."

One of the men, poised to bite the sandwich in his hand, glanced up. "You that Manhattan guy who called me?"

I nodded.

"How long's this gonna take? These fellas are pretty foolish with their money, see, and I might need ten, fifteen minutes to clean them out completely."

The other men barely noticed. They'd heard the shtick, it seemed. The phone rang. Weaver picked it up with his unoccupied hand. He listened. "All right, I'm coming over there." He put the phone down and talked toward his sandwich before he bit it: "Alva needs to get her pills picked up. So I gotta go. I'll be back in a couple of hands. Sammy, don't eat my pickle. You"—he pointed to me—"come with me while I gotta go do this. I'll drive."

Indeed he would. Behind the dry cleaner, pulled into a tight driveway, rested a green Cadillac with an old MCCAIN FOR PRESIDENT sticker on the spotless bumper. We settled inside, and I noticed a box of Cuban cigars sloppily taped to the dashboard of the expensive car.

Weaver handed me his sandwich and pulled a tiny pair of

scissors out of his breast pocket. "Hold that, I have to smoke." He pulled a cigar out of the box, snipped the end, and lit it. "You know Floral Park?"

"No," I said, inspecting the sandwich with interest.

"Then you get the tour." Away we went. "So you talked to old Doc Greenfeld, and he sent you my direction."

"He told me Roger Corbett was trying to—"

"See that place?" Weaver pointed his cigar at a gas station packed with cars pumping gas. "Coulda bought that one in 1974 for twenty-three thousand, what an idiot I was, thought it was a risky deal. What did I know? Anyways, yes, the kid, he wanted all the old dope on his father, put me in a hell of a jam."

"Why?"

"Ah, geez, here I am, eighty-four years old, and along comes this Roger, calls me up and says, You knew my father a long time ago, please tell me all his private secrets." Weaver's eyes became more animated, and he jerked his hand toward a fast-food franchise. "That place, the lease is coming up, the owner wants them out."

We drove on another minute.

"So you were saying," I prompted him, "about the secrets?"

"Right, right, so he wants to know all these things, and of course, this raises lots of questions, okay? Why didn't the father tell the son, why didn't the mother tell the son? And if old Willie Corbett was still alive, what would he want me to say? See, I'm just an old man trying to remember where I put my hearing aids, and now I'm supposed to communicate with dead people?" He looked at me, wide-eyed, as if I were the source of his problem. "Well, listen up, mister, it bothers me, got that?"

As we drove up the avenue, his mind worked the landscape, again distracting him. "See that FOR SALE sign? I know the owner, Frankie Phelan. He got himself one of these adjustable-rate mortgages. You know what I think about when I hear the word *adjustable*?"

"Uh, no."

"I think about those pants that came out back in the sixties, when Lyndon Johnson was president, that had elastic in the waistband, they adjusted to your stomach. As you got fatter, they kept adjusting. So that's— See? There's another one, that one there! Frankie owns that one, too, he borrowed too much off of it and used the money to buy condos in Miami that hadn't been built yet. Six of them, six mortgages. Now he can't sell them! Pow! Right in the kisser! He made an *adjustment,* heh, he adjusted to starvation."

I was beginning to feel that Weaver was playing with me. "So what'd you tell Roger Corbett?"

He glared at me. "I says: You wanna know what I know about your old man? Fine. But you won't like it, young fella. I says, I knew your father back when he was a fresh banana, before he got married, back in 1950-whatever-it-was, and okay, so, number one, he started his fancy Manhattan law firm by winning eighteen thousand dollars in a poker game held on a fishing boat out in Greenport, Long Island, and I should know because I was the guy counting cards for him on the other side of the table. We had a system we'd practiced for weeks. We coulda gotten killed for that if they'd caught us. Woulda fucking served us right, too. Bunch of grade-A chumps. So number two, I says, your father had to keep his dick wet, you know what I mean? He had at least one child out of wedlock, maybe more, after he got married. For people of a certain background, okay, that kind of thing was considered pretty shocking back then. Roger-boy really wanted to know about *that*, of course. Did I remember who it was, boy or girl, and so on and so forth, and I says no, no, I never met any of Willie's female acquaintances, but I knew he made payments for child support, maybe there were some old records in his papers somewhere, maybe—Wait, I love that place!" Weaver waved his cigar at a low commercial building. "I owned it *twice*, sold it in eighty-seven, market was topping out, bought it back in ninety-three maybe, sold it again in 2004, that was a real—"

Weaver stopped in midthought. We drifted along. He smiled to himself. Or maybe it was a gassy grimace.

"You were saying?"

He looked across the Cadillac seat and seemed surprised to find me there. "Oh, yes, waitaminute . . . the poker game, yes, the bastard kids out of wedlock, then, oh, the third thing was that Willie once admitted he was no good at running his own blasted law firm and that in the early days the firm was actually run by his secretary. What the hell, right? Hotshot law firm run by the boss's secretary? On the q.t., of course. He won the big cases, but she ran the actual operation. Told him who to hire and fire. This went on for a good ten years. Willie mighta been banging her, too, for all I know! Woman was a genius with legal strategy, too. Her name shoulda been on the firm's letterhead, you know what I'm sayin'? She sat in all the meetings taking notes, then afterward they'd talk. The other partners wouldn't give her the time of day, but she was the one Willie discussed everything with."

I'd worked in the last days of Wilson Corbett's regime. "A woman named Anna Hewes?"

"I wouldn't remember, but anyway, I says these things to Roger." Weaver shook his head. "Think of it. 'Your father had at least one other child you don't know about, your father got the money he used to start his law firm by illegal gambling, and he really wasn't the one who made it so successful.' A lot to swallow. But if he don't like it, tough toenails."

I didn't see how this information fit into what I'd learned about Roger Corbett. "I know this sounds a little crazy, but did Roger ever say anything about Christmas ornaments or about his Czech girlfriend?"

"What? Christmas in Czechoslovakia? I don't know what you're talking about. It was all about his father." Weaver looked at me, his manner gentler now. "Something I've learned, see, is that one of the things men think about as they get older is they really want to know who their father was."

The next morning, I slipped into my pocket the two crudely fashioned Christmas ornaments that I'd taken from the boxes in storage, made a detour on my way to work, and climbed the stairs to Diamond District Assaying and Smelting Inc. on Forty-seventh Street between Fifth and Sixth. There I rang the bell. We've had a few cases involving businesses that buy and sell precious metals, and the thing to remember about them is that they don't create anything; they must quickly sell whatever they buy, lest the ever-volatile spot prices run against them. It's a big-volume-and-small-margin business. Fraudulent insurance claims by these businesses are rarely related to fire, because structure fires don't destroy gold or silver. Theft, of course, is another matter.

The door led to a small, windowless room that contained a table with a plastic tray on it, a security camera, and another door. In the middle of the room stood a standard airport-style metal detector. Now the intercom panel on the wall crackled. "Yes?" came a voice.

"I'm here to—"

"Take off your coat."

I took off my coat.

"What metal do you have?"

"I don't know," I said to the room.

"Don't know?"

"I'm guessing silver."

"Put your silver in the tray."

I did this. The ornaments looked even more pathetic than before.

"Now step forward, slowly, through the metal detector."

I did this.

"Retrieve your metals."

The second door buzzed, and I pushed through it, holding my coat and the ornaments. This room was not much larger. A man in a leather jacket stood before me. He had gold rings on every finger, a gold watch, and a thick gold medallion around his neck.

"Please, arms up. Just a formality."

He waved a security wand under my arms, between my legs, down my chest, along my arms.

"We didn't used to have to be so careful, but every year or two somebody gets courageous, and then there's a problem."

He waved me over to the counter. "You have silver?"

I held out the ornaments. He looked at them. Shook his head.

"Not silver." He put them down on the counter. "Doesn't feel right. Maybe there is a little silver mixed in, maybe not."

"What is it?"

"We'll let the machine tell us, okay? We'll assay this and determine the composition. If this metal turns out to be twenty-five cents' worth of aluminum, you still pay the assay charge, understand?"

"Yes."

He pulled out a tray from the machine, placed the ornaments on it, and slid the tray back into the machine.

"What is that?" I asked.

"X-ray fluorescence. The machine is a wavelength disper-sive spectrometer. We're bombarding the sample with X-rays and measuring the resulting energy. Do you know any chem-istry, about electron transitions?"

"No."

"This machine is very accurate. Measures the composition of almost any sample."

A computer monitor flickered numbers and letters—signs of elements, I guessed.

"No silver." He blinked at the readout, studied it more closely. "Interesting. Where did you get this sample?"

I have a pretty good stare when I really need it. "That's a long story."

He nodded. "You'd like to sell us this sample?"

"What is it?"

"It is an alloy of cheap steel and a fine metal called rhodium."

"Valuable?"

"I will gladly tell you, but first I want to check with my boss about something." He retreated to the far end of the counter and picked up a phone. I studied the spot-price screen behind the counter for anything that looked like rhodium but saw nothing. Gold and platinum were bouncing around, though, as the professional commodities speculators tried to gauge the future price of oil, the dollar, and who knows what else.

Down the counter the man nodded and hung up. "The boss, he says we do not usually pay out on this metal."

"Oh."

"But he asks if there's more. If you have more he'll pay for this."

"I know where there's quite a bit more."

"Just like this, same composition?"

"Yes."

"In that case we will pay, so that you will bring us more." He pushed a button on his computer. The screen changed. "Price is down a little this morning. We've got here about 6.47 ounces of low-quality steel, which has no value at all, maybe one penny, no more, and for the rhodium, which assays out to 2.36 ounces, I'll pay you spot minus nine percent."

"Maybe I should sell it elsewhere, get closer to market price."

"Sir, rhodium is an industrial metal, and it is sold in refined form such as finished ingots or spooled wire to big companies. That is what market price means. Your sample of rhodium is mixed in with junk metal. Why, I do not know and"—he glanced at me over his glasses—"why, I am not asking. It needs to be smelted, which is a very expensive, messy process. The smelters that recover rhodium are big operations. We are just middlemen. They don't pay us spot, you can be sure."

This sounded plausible. "So what's the current price per ounce?"

He pointed at a board of flickering numbers. "That would be, today, three minutes ago, $9,416 per ounce."

Impossible. "Per ounce?"

"Yes."

Minus 9 percent, about $8,500 an ounce. I felt my blood pressure rise, one of the many new sensations that comes to you in middle age.

"Cash or check?"

A check created an eternal record.

"Cash."

He brought a banded stack of new hundreds out of his drawer, tore off the band, and put it into a cash-counting machine. Then he pulled two tens, a single, and some change from a cash drawer. "This is $20,221.80. Do you wish to count?"

"No."

He placed the cash into an envelope and taped the receipt to the outside.

"Please sign."

I signed as illegibly as possible.

He held the envelope up to a small video camera. "Please

state your name, the date, the amount, and then say, 'I have been paid in full and all accounts are fully settled to my complete satisfaction.'"

I repeated this statement to the camera.

"Thank you."

A minute later I was walking along the street with the huge wad of cash in my breast pocket. When I got to my office, I couldn't resist opening the envelope and staring at the bills. They had that new-money smell, too. I slipped the envelope into my desk drawer. Twenty thousand bucks for a couple of crummy Christmas ornaments. Who knew? Not Roger Corbett, nor his wife, who had paid movers to take the stuff from his place to the storage facility. The storage unit downtown had five heavy boxes of these ornaments. A fortune. Millions, even! They didn't rightfully belong to Roger Corbett's estate or his wife or his mother, they certainly didn't belong to me, and it was questionable if they'd ever legally belonged to Eliska Sedlacek. Had they been stolen by her Russian boyfriend, Nikolai Gamov? That seemed likely, but how was I to find that out? Call up the Russian consulate? Ask around Moscow?

That was the wrong question, though. The right question was this: Who other than Eliska Sedlacek knew I had access to the boxes, and what bad things were they willing to do to get them back?

eight

A GENIUS CHUMP

Each of us, I suspect, has a private list of the stupidest things we've ever done. Our most self-destructive, deluded, or hurtful actions. I wish, for example, that I hadn't listened to the cancer doctors who told me they could save my mother's life. She underwent several unnecessary operations that made her suffer. Had she not been dealing with the operations, we might've had a chance to look over her life together those few last weeks. She would've liked that, and doing so would've helped me, too. Instead, something else quite different happened, which I don't like to remember. Agreeing to those operations is the top item on my list, and now and then I drink a little too much wine and go over that decision, to no effect.

Nonetheless, one of the few consolations of middle age has been that my list has not changed that much in the last five years. But now I was wondering if my willingness to find out what had happened to Roger Corbett was becoming one of the more stupid things I'd done in a while. And maybe I'd agreed to do this because my life had become so utterly predictable. Yes. *Admit it,* I told myself, *you have a deeply boring life, George, and you took this assignment hoping you'd get to do something unexpected.*

What should I do next, move the boxes elsewhere? Given that Eliska didn't know where they were, that wouldn't change things much. I could tell Roger's ailing mother, Mrs. Corbett, or his ex-wife, Valerie, about the boxes, but that simply placed them on the list of people who knew about them, potentially endangering them, and it might put me in the position of being forced to identify them. I could, it was true, turn the whole matter over to the authorities, especially my wife's local contacts in the Justice Department, but that would become a dangerous entanglement itself. It could end up involving me working on behalf of the FBI or the NYPD to snare someone, leading to my becoming a witness in court. I'd have to hire my own lawyer for guidance. My name would get dragged into a story that featured not just a man killed by a garbage truck and a mysterious Czech hand model but a fortune hidden inside a Manhattan storage unit. Hey, throw in the Russian mobsters, too. Tabloid heaven! My law firm would look very unfavorably upon such a development, and surely the firm would have to answer the worried inquiries from our sole client, the European insurance company. Even worse, my wife would end up having to explain my involvement to her superiors at her bank, even submit to a rake-through of our finances. Not good. No, I thought, better to seek the elegant solution that gets you out of this situation quickly and cleanly forever.

I was mulling all this one night as I watched the Yankees game with the sound turned off and the radio turned on. I prefer hearing John Sterling on WCBS-AM call the game, even though he's corny as hell. My wife saw me staring out the window, ignoring the game.

"George," Carol said, "what're you thinking about?"

The woman's intuition was scary.

"Not much, the price of rice in China, things like that."

Carol waited to see if I might say something more, but when I didn't, she flicked her attention back to the game.

The next morning, as soon as I arrived at work, I asked our law school intern Ethan Randolph to come into my office. He's a big, bright kid, and if we were smart we would hire him after graduation, maybe first cleaning out some of the lazies and crazies or even dumping the wormwood partners who are no longer productive so every level of the firm could ratchet up a spot or two.

Ethan works hard and people like him right away—the kind of young man who you want to help with his career. I told Ethan I needed a quick research job. "Rhodium," I said. "What is it, who has it, why is it so valuable? I don't want a polite memo, I want the one-page cheat sheet."

At noon, I slipped out, telling Laura, my assistant, that I had a doctor's appointment. At age twenty-nine, she has reached the Age of Terrifying Indecision, which is to say her boyfriend seems neither interested in marriage, which bothers her, nor particularly worth marrying, which bothers her even more. My spies tell me that when I'm out of the office she launches into complex discussions of the Boyfriend Problem with her girlfriends on the phone and by e-mail simultaneously. All this is to say that I knew she wouldn't be attentive to my absence—a good thing, given whom I was going to visit.

I don't know why exactly Staten Island got a bad name; maybe it's because two generations of New Yorkers going to the Jersey Shore in the summer took Route 440 to the Outerbridge Crossing to avoid the turnpike and thereby went past the infamous Fresh Kills landfill, which still smells bad, years after the city closed it. Even today, Staten Island is seen as hopelessly parochial and tribal and lowbrow. This attitude has always amused me, because there's a lot of smart, quiet money on Staten Island.

I zoomed out across the Verrazano Bridge. Then I slipped off 278 at Exit 12, making a left at the underpass to get to Todt Hill Road. The road winds upward into the woods, the price and size of the houses rising along the way. If you want to live in a seven-thousand-square-foot mansion beneath large trees and still call yourself a resident of New York City, the homes off Todt Hill Road are a pretty good place to do it. They are not just mansions but fortresses: generally made of stone or brick, boxy, imposing, and meant to guard their inhabitants, like my friend Anthony G.

Anthony has made several fortunes: in his father's heating-oil business (muscled out some of the competition in Brooklyn and Queens, increasing his market share), in the cement-truck business (knows how to bid on the big Manhattan construction jobs), and in the metropolitan wholesale-window business (escaped the federal indictments in the nineties). In the 1970s, when he was a fat kid from Staten Island with an attitude, he and I went to summer camp together just south of Binghamton. I was his only real pal that summer. Our friendship has lasted, despite his various legal troubles. We have lunch every year or two. The talk is never of business but of wives, children, parents.

When I got within fifty yards of Anthony's house, I stopped and checked my BlackBerry. Ethan's report was waiting for me:

Rhodium (Rh) is a very scarce precious metal, part of the platinum group, and is used in industrial applications and for electroplating jewelry. Highly resistant to corrosion and oxidation. Mined as a primary product in South Africa (vast preponderance of metric tons produced annually), and in Canada and Russia as nickel by-product. One large deposit in Montana. Automobile sector consumes 85 percent of production, mostly in catalytic converters. Booming consumption of cars in China and India ensures future value. Rhodium is so valuable that catalytic converters are routinely sold on eBay for salvage. Converter scrap is collected globally and most shipped back to South Africa for recycling. All mining and smelting processes highly toxic to environment. Salvage industry fragmented and highly competitive at local level but coalesces into several main global players that buy and recycle scrap. Price moves somewhat independently of gold and other precious metal commodities, and even somewhat independently of auto manufacturing cycles. May have new medical technology uses in future, potentially in blood-gas filtering applications. Very secretive demand in research quantities by major pharmaceutical R & D divisions. Expensive to refine, demand always high. Although big global wholesale players dominate, smaller players want in. Some evidence of crude recycling efforts in Russian and various Asian countries. Local exchange of raw opium for scrap rhodium discovered by CIA in Afghanistan, 2006. Rhodium scrap traded for AK-47s in Somalia, 2007. Illegal diamond traders familiar with rhodium beads, Interpol, 2005. Smuggling increasing because metal is fungible globally; wherever cars are salvaged, rhodium has street value. Can be bonded with other metals for concealment. Mines with high rhodium content in South Africa are patrolled by armed guards. Recent price as high as $9,400 an ounce.

I stared at the screen, feeling ill. Behind whoever wanted those boxes of metal ornaments burned a furious global demand.

You can't see Anthony's house from the road. His driveway passes behind high hedges of arborvitae into a cobblestone courtyard area. I pulled in and waited, as he'd told me to do when I'd called him earlier. A door next to the garage opened, and a young man came out.

"You George Young?"

I nodded.

"Can you prove it?"

I had my U.S. passport in my breast pocket for this very reason. He inspected it, looked at me, inspected it again.

"I got older," I said.

Not even a smile. "Please leave the keys in the car."

I got out, and he silently frisked me. This wasn't a pleasant feeling. He found my BlackBerry.

"It's Mr. Anthony's personal preference that cell phones and all other electronic devices remain in the car."

"Not a problem," I said.

"Please turn it off."

"Also not a problem."

"No other devices in the car?"

"No," I said.

"You are sure?"

"Would I lie to you?"

He could have smiled, but he didn't.

I followed the man into the garage and down a plain hallway into an enormous kitchen. Tuscan floor tiles, brushed-steel gas stoves, the whole nine yards. An older woman with her hair in a bun was chopping tomatoes. I smelled basil and some kind of cheese, too.

I was taken out to a terrace. Anthony was sitting in a teak lawn chair reading *The Wall Street Journal,* and before he turned his head I saw the years on him now; he was sophisticated, wealthy, careful, and safer than he'd ever been before, which in his case meant a lot.

"George, so nice you dropped by."

I smiled, shook his hand. "Thanks for seeing me, Anthony."

We took a walk in the woods, and I explained about Roger Corbett, Eliska Sedlacek, the metal items she'd smuggled into the country, her murdered boyfriend, the time I was followed in my cab, the fact that Roger Corbett's phone was still in service, and last, the enormous value of the rhodium.

"I'm starting to feel like I'm in a jam," I said.

Anthony nodded. He knew about jams, had gotten out of most of them. "They want that rhodium stuff," he said, "and sooner or later they'll come and get it. But what do they have that you want?"

"I want them to leave me and all of my ancestors alone for the next five hundred years."

"Goes without saying."

"The only other thing that I want is of no value to them." I explained about Roger Corbett's cell phone bill, how it had the number of the last call he made.

"Why do you think they have it?"

"Like I said, the line is still operative. The ex-wife doesn't really know what happened to the bills and so on, where they are. She wasn't paying attention. His stuff, his mail and everything, was all mixed up with the girlfriend, and she's connected to these guys somehow. She's nervous about something. Somebody is paying the bill, keeping his phone alive."

"Which might have value to them," said Anthony. "Might mean they're using it. Which could implicate them in some way, too."

"But Roger Corbett had the phone when he was hit. Although I haven't heard anything about it being found where he was killed."

Anthony shook his head. "If the EMS or cops found it on him, it would have been returned. If the phone flew away from him, it could easily have been run over by a car, picked up by a street cleaner, whatever. Maybe someone picked it up, used it until the battery ran out, then chucked it. But that wouldn't have stopped these guys, they could've gotten another one— that's not tough, so long as they had a bill. And so if they're using the phone, they won't want to give you a bill from it."

"I don't want any bill, I just want the bill that shows the call that Corbett made before he died."

"That's all you want, that one piece of paper? You don't want the rhodium?"

"Of course I want it, but it's not mine."

Anthony shook his head. I could see he didn't like how messy and ill-defined the situation was, conjecture piled atop conjecture. "You know, George, the situation is more complicated than you understand," he said. "I got to think about this. Got to look at it from their point of view. They know you've got nothing to do with this whole setup. You're just some goof who stumbled into this. But let me tell you, one of those guys is thinking about it all the time. He's thinking: This George Young guy is a goof, he has the keys to a big wad of money, maybe doesn't even know it, how do we make him do what we want? This guy is thinking about this constantly, George. He's like me. His mind chews away at it. He's going to know where you live, what you do, what your phone number is. Maybe he's done his homework, knows your wife is connected to law-enforcement people. He wants to stay away from that. He'd rather do this the easy way, let you catch yourself for them somehow."

I nodded miserably.

"Does the Czech girl know that the Christmas ornaments are made of rhodium, worth whatever it is, eight, nine thou an ounce?"

"She knows the stuff is valuable, because she smuggled it into the country, but whether she knows what it actually is—I don't know. She could, easily enough."

We climbed the path toward Anthony's house. Our feet whisked through dry leaves.

"Anthony, what would you do if *you* were looking to get your twenty pounds of stolen rhodium back?"

"And you're my guy? I find out your vulnerability, and then I grab you and make you go and get those boxes for me. In and out in a few hours. You take the boxes somewhere I can't be detected, I get them from you, then make you go away."

"What do you mean, make me go away?"

"I mean I threaten you so badly that you'll never tell anyone."

"Wouldn't it be less risky to bury me in some shallow unmarked grave?"

"Not really. You're a lawyer, your wife is a bank compliance officer, you guys know people. All that stuff would just make an investigation a certainty. They don't want that. Besides, once they get the rhodium, they can get out of the country quickly. They want the boxes and to be on a plane the same day."

We worked our way back to the patio.

Anthony had the answer now. I could see it in his eyes.

"Wait, George, this is what you do. You need the game changer, the unexpected thing that rewires all the incentives. You call up this Czech girl and just give her the boxes of ornaments back, like you have no idea at all what they're worth, and then take a little vacation. Tell her you're going to the Jersey Shore, whatever, and then instead get lost, a week or two in Nova Scotia or someplace. That way you give everybody plenty of time to do whatever they need to do and get out of the country, and everybody figures you were a chump."

"Be a chump and they'll let me alone."

"No, a genius chump."

"What about the cell phone bill?"

"Forget about it."

"I don't want to forget about it."

"It's a cell phone bill." He looked at me, then pointed to his head. "Be a *genius* chump, George. Not just a regular one."

We said good-bye. I was shown to my car. It had been washed.

Traffic was heavy on 278 back into Brooklyn. Being a genius chump now seemed like a very good idea. As I sat in my car, I dialed Eliska Sedlacek. I'd tell her I'd get the boxes to her the next day, no questions asked. I wouldn't even mention Roger Corbett's cell phone bill. In and out, then done.

The call rang, then picked up: "This is Eliska. I am on modeling job out of United States. Please you leave message."

I hung up. She could be outside the United States or maybe not. Traffic began to move, and soon I was on the Verrazano Bridge back to Brooklyn. Next, I called the Blue Curtain Lounge. Maybe the bartender I'd spoken with before had already come into work, though it was early. I called. He picked up, and I recognized his voice.

"You remember me? I gave you my card."

"Sure, sure. You called me Mort."

If he saw the Czech hand model, please call me right away, I said.

"Okay," he replied, laughing.

"What's so funny?"

"I told you she was trouble."

"Well, you were right," I said, the hazy spires of Manhattan off to my left. "More than you know."

nine

PARTY ANIMALS

I was anxious, and when I'm anxious, I can't sleep. I think too much, I hear my wife snore softly (oh, the accommodations one makes as the years of marriage go by), I hear the traffic on West End Avenue outside our apartment. I get up and prowl around the living room, doing nothing in particular, read the paper, eat an unnecessary bowl of cereal, read the out-of-town box scores on the Internet. A stupid misery. And by this point I was anxious all the time, my sleep burned away to not much more than a few cheap hours before daylight. I'd tried earplugs and over-the-counter sleeping pills, but they didn't help much. Sooner or later, I told myself, the guys who'd threatened Eliska Sedlacek would find me and demand I produce five boxes of rhodium trinkets. But with her out of touch, I had no move to make, no way to be the genius chump.

The following Monday I was talking on the phone with our local counsel in Tallahassee, Florida, about the case in which the claimant probably sank his own yacht on purpose when Anna Hewes knocked on my door.

"Mrs. Corbett wants to talk with you."

Anna had helped get me into this mess in the first place, and I was a little curt with her. "Just tell her I'll call her back."

"I don't think you understand. She's here. In the reception area."

"This really isn't a—" I stopped myself. "Bring her in."

Which Anna did, in a wheelchair and with a nurse, who got Mrs. Corbett settled, then left. Mrs. Corbett had put on her makeup and pearls for the visit, and sat in the wheelchair expectantly, her hands gripping both armrests.

"Quite a surprise." I rose from my desk and shook her hand. It felt cold. She looked at me with overt impatience, as if I'd been keeping her waiting.

"I felt I needed to see you, Mr. Young."

Mrs. Corbett seemed a little breathy in her speech, and the swelling around her ankles appeared worse than before. "I would've been happy to speak by phone," I said, "if you'd called."

She waved a bony hand back at the hallway. "I see they remodeled my husband's office."

"Yes, we redid the whole floor a few years ago."

Mrs. Corbett spied the desk photo of my wife and daughter. "Seems you have a happy life, George."

"Mrs. Corbett, please tell me why you've come to see me."

"The doctors keep making me wait for my heart operation. But they could call me anytime. I want to know what you've found out about Roger. It's been weeks now, Mr. Young."

What could I tell her? Not much, I decided. "I met with the private investigator, who gave me the name of the super of the building where your son lived. He put me onto your son's girlfriend."

Mrs. Corbett paddled her feet angrily in her wheelchair. "He didn't have a girlfriend. Not Roger. He was still very much in love with Valerie."

The point wasn't worth arguing over. "It seems that Roger's career began to get, well—like a lot of people's—a little bumpy in his late forties."

"That's putting it nicely," she snapped.

"I was trying to put it nicely."

Mrs. Corbett peered at me with irritation. "Roger got too ambitious. He had a beautiful life, the house on the water in Mamaroneck. I think he coached his son's teams. But that doesn't have much to do with the night he died."

I didn't have time for this conversation. "Okay, I know he sat in the bar downtown waiting to make a phone call. The bartender remembers he made the call and wrote something down. I'm trying to get the phone bill that will tell me. Meanwhile, I've spoken to some people who Roger was—"

But Mrs. Corbett wasn't listening. "I'm having this operation sooner or later now, Mr. Young, and I need something to hang on to before they put me under." She stared at me ferociously, somehow sensing that I was holding back on her. "My husband gave you *your life* here, and he picked you right out of some crummy job in Queens when—"

"And I'm very grateful," I interrupted. "I've been trying to—"

"I am *insisting* that you find me an answer before I—"

The nurse reappeared, perhaps having heard Mrs. Corbett's strident voice. The nurse bent close to whisper something to Mrs. Corbett, who then shook her head. "I *will*, as soon as I'm done saying what I have to say." She looked up at me. "Is there anything you can tell me, anything at all?"

"I told you he had a girlfriend, but you didn't believe me."

She shook her head in disgust. "Some woman may have been sharing her *charms* with my son, but I doubt it meant anything to him. He was lonely, that's all. She probably thought Roger had some money. But he didn't, since he gave every penny to his wife and children."

"After they sold the house on Cove Road in Mamaroneck?"

"As part of the divorce, yes."

"Did you know your son contacted Charlie Weaver, your husband's old friend?"

"No, I didn't," Mrs. Corbett said, her voice holding more interest now.

"He lives out in Floral Park. He shared an apartment with your husband as a young man. I believe Roger asked him some very personal questions about Mr. Corbett . . ." I had to be careful here, not knowing if she knew of her husband's infidelity, the child he'd fathered out of wedlock, according to Weaver. "And I think your son got some answers he wasn't expecting."

Mrs. Corbett munched her mouth once or twice as if she wanted to say something but could not.

"Did your husband have secrets that would've upset Roger?" I asked directly now.

"If he did, then he was just like anyone else," she answered. "But frankly it is *not* my late husband I'm interested in, Mr. Young. It's— I miss my son Roger terribly." At this, an awful phlegm-strangled cry caught in her throat. "And I just want to know what happened. Please, I don't have much time left. *Please.*"

She seemed suddenly exhausted by this declaration and slumped in her wheelchair, eyes downcast. Her nurse nodded at me, signaling Mrs. Corbett was done, then pushed her out of my office.

I sat at my desk, staring distractedly at the spill of papers on it. Why was life so messy? Why did I feel I had disappointed Mrs. Corbett, and what, really, could I do about it?

That night I was brushing my teeth and getting ready for bed when the phone rang. My wife answered, then called me. It was the bartender from the Blue Curtain Lounge.

"What's up?"

"That freaky hand-model girl is here." Eliska Sedlacek. "She and her friends are headed uptown to some kind of party. You said to call you if I saw her."

I thanked him. "They say where they're going?"

"Not exactly, but I heard the corner. It's 109th and Lex."

"They left yet?"

"Just on their way, taking a cab, I bet."

I could get there before them, I realized. "You're positive?"

"No, I'm not drop-dead positive. But I'm pretty sure."

I hung up and looked at my watch. It was a few minutes after eleven. A cab from Elizabeth Street going uptown to 109th and Lex would probably go by way of Third Avenue. Even hitting all the lights, it would take fifteen minutes. I could go downstairs, walk over to Broadway, and be there a lot faster, crossing Central Park at 96th and going uptown on Madison, right on 110th, then making a right onto Lex. Even if they walked west to the uptown 6 train, which would be easier, they'd be getting off at the 110th Street stop. I could beat that, too.

I'd been calling Eliska for about a week, with no answer, left messages. Maybe she was just avoiding me. Well, no longer. I was sick of waiting for something to happen.

"I'm going out," I said to Carol.

"Why?"

"It has to do with Mrs. Corbett."

"You're kidding, right?"

I pulled on my shoes or, rather, Roger's shoes. "I'm not kidding, actually."

"You mind telling me what all this is?"

I looked at my watch. I had to assume Eliska and her companions had decided to take the subway. "I'll tell you when I get back."

"When will that be? The last time you ran out like this you came back hours later, bombed out of your mind. You going to do that again?"

"I don't know what I'm going to do."

"You think I like this?"

"I think it really bothers you. Makes you nuts."

"So? Doesn't that matter?"

Carol was right to be furious. But I said, "I have to go. I apologize categorically. Please don't stay up for me."

"This is really—"

The obscenity was the one she usually used. I grabbed my wallet and keys and headed to the door.

Carol followed me. "That's it?" she cried. "Just fly out into the night, no explanation?"

"No. Sorry."

"Take a raincoat, it looks like it could start."

I hurriedly grabbed one from the hallway, and as I waited for the elevator on our floor, our neighbor, Mrs. Conaway, came back from the garbage chute with her empty trash can. She gave me a look that suggested she'd heard my wife's unhappy voice.

I walked over to Broadway, caught a cab, and headed east. My cell phone rang. It was the bartender again. "I thought I'd also mention that the girl's had a lot to drink," he said.

"When'd they leave?"

"Five minutes ago, maybe."

"Any chance they were taking the subway?"

"I don't know if she could walk that far."

I thanked him and hung up. Then the phone rang again.

"In quite a hurry, George!" Carol yelled. "You took *my* rain-coat!" We had matching ones, blue.

I turned off my phone. Soon I was at the corner of 109th and Lexington. I found a bodega where I could stand and watch the intersection. It wasn't the greatest neighborhood in the world. A zone of stickups, fires, and assorted illicit activities. If you wanted to open a business here, your premiums would have to reflect the neighborhood's added risk.

Five minutes later a cab eased along 109th Street, pulled over, and stopped. Three women got out, Eliska among them, easily recognizable not only by her willowy height but also by her dark gloves, which contrasted with the paleness of her arms under the streetlights.

I followed them. The young women stopped halfway down the block, consulted a piece of paper, then stepped inside a doorway. I could hear music coming from the open windows directly above, several floors up, bouncing off the opposite building. The pulsing hum of a party. I lingered twenty feet away, wondering what to do. Another cab pulled up, and more young people piled out and went straight for the door. They looked self-important and low-rent glamorous. Then a foursome rounded the corner and barged confidently right in.

So it was a big party. Could I get inside?

You're an old guy going gray, I told myself, *you'll seem like you don't belong.* I put on my wife's raincoat. Not a good fit. Something was in the pocket. Her sunglasses, from her walks along Riverside Drive. Then I floated back down the block into the bodega.

Some kids were buying donuts. They all wore baseball caps.

"Hey, guys," I said. "I need to buy a baseball cap."

"We ain't sellin'."

"I'm paying twenty bucks."

"For nothin', mister."

"Forty."

That changed their attitude. I chose from a Yankees cap, a Raiders cap, and something called Uptown Diesel Records, with red lettering. I chose that one.

"That one's extra. Sixty, six-oh."

I paid. I stuck the cap on, then slipped on my wife's sunglasses, and checked myself out in the reflection of the bodega's window.

I looked ridiculous. And yet . . . potentially legitimate. I went back to the door that Eliska and her two companions had used, buzzed, then pushed through. Two enormous guys stood inside, each talking on a phone. I nodded matter-of-factly at them.

"Wait."

I stopped.

"Who you?"

I saw no master invite list. "I'm from the management company."

"What management company?" said one of the big boys.

I just stared at him in my funky sunglasses and waited.

"Cool." He pointed to the door.

I rode up in an elevator with three more young women and a well-dressed young man who'd recently invested in hair plugs. I tried not to stare at their uniform rows. Meanwhile, the girls discussed places to buy shoes in the Village. They seemed to be tolerating Mr. Hair Plugs. The elevator stopped, and we exited into an enormous room boiling with people. I hadn't been to a party like this in twenty-five years. I smelled cigarettes, pot, booze, maybe hashish. The room was dark, and I sensed the space went back and back and back, with music coming from somewhere, and clusters of tables to the sides, several open bars. I kept my wife's sunglasses on, as if that mattered.

It took me more than thirty minutes to find Eliska. She was sitting on a long sofa, dressed in heels and a short green dress, smoking a cigarette with her gloves on and talking with another woman. I watched from the side, making sure she didn't see me. Her long dark hair was piled on top of her head, several strands loose. Fetching, that. Then I worked my way around behind her, getting close enough to hear what she was saying.

Something to do with Prague, the music scene there, or some such. Then the modeling scene in Paris, then London, then a certain kind of shampoo that was hard to get unless you knew the right people. It was all a tad drunkenly insipid. I listened for another five minutes, my mind wandering a bit. But then Eliska said, "I move back there, soon as I can, maybe next week I hope."

"Why?"

Yes, why? I thought. *Is it because your boyfriends keep ending up dead?*

"This country, I thought I wanted to live in America, but it's too much stress."

No surprise. I took off my wife's sunglasses and walked around the sofa.

"Well, hello," I said to Eliska.

She frowned at me, and I worried that she might angrily sense I'd tracked her to the party. "Mr. Young? What you do here?"

"I thought I might find you," I said evasively.

Eliska smiled dreamily. "So funny to run into you." She was drunk, yes. "So, this is my friend, Mr. Young," she told her friend, then looked back at me. "I thought it was going to be good party, but I am wrong, I think. You know . . ." She picked up her drink from the floor, drank it off, then stared at me.

"Yes?"

"Your raincoat is too small."

"Yes."

She rose unsteadily, and in her heels she was tall enough that our eyes were at the same level. "Now I am done. Will you get me cab?"

We walked outside and to the corner of Lexington Avenue. It took a while, but a cab finally arrived. I opened the door. She hopped in.

"Well?" Eliska called.

"What?"

"Aren't you getting in, too?"

I got in. Eliska leaned forward and gave the cabbie her address on Broome Street—which was also Roger Corbett's last address.

"It is strange thing that I run into you at this party," she mused, lighting another cigarette and throwing the match out the window. "You know anyone there?"

"Not really."

"I knew few people, something to do with a new movie, I think."

We were quiet as the cab raced downtown. She tugged habitually at the wrists of her gloves, keeping them tight. The smell of her perfume and the cigarette filled the cab.

"So, listen," I began, "I need to talk to you about—"

"Just a minute." Eliska pulled out her phone, dialed, said something in what sounded like Czech. She spoke quickly, voice animated. This made me tense, and she seemed to understand that. "This is just girlfriend, she move here and I am having brunch with her on Sunday."

Did I believe this? Maybe. I needed to tell her that I'd get the boxes of rhodium trinkets to her the next morning and in such a way that did not reveal I knew their astounding value. Then I'd drop her at her apartment building before whisking back up to the West Side. And the next day, once I had transferred the boxes to her, we'd have nothing more to do with each other, and she'd deliver the boxes to whoever wanted them. But Eliska slumped in her seat, seemingly dazed by the long night of drinking, and I felt wary of pressing her with a plan. It seemed likely that in her state she wouldn't remember any arrangements we made.

The cab rolled to a stop on Broome Street. "All right, listen," I began. "I'm going to call you in the morning and discuss—"

"Wait, George, no, we talk now about everything," she slurred as she opened the taxi door. "I am not too drunk, I promise. I drink coffee, and it will be fine."

"You're sure?"

"Yes, of course." She swung her long legs out to the street. "Aren't you coming inside with me?"

I took a deep breath. The hour was late, the circumstances questionable. *Don't assume anything,* I told myself. I remembered her trailing her fingers along my cheek, how I'd known Roger Corbett had felt those same fingers himself. I wondered if perhaps someone might be waiting upstairs, the same man or men she said had threatened her. And she'd just made a brief call to someone and spoken in Czech. *Don't do it,* I thought.

"George?" came her voice. "Are you coming now?"

I reached for my wallet to pay the cabbie. "Yes, I'm coming."

ten

LONG NIGHT, SHORT MORNING

I genuinely did not mind walking behind Eliska up the stairs of her building. "I'm a *little* drunk," she announced playfully. "Not that much, just some." She turned back to gaze at me, and all the reserve she'd previously displayed drained away, her true saucy abandon freed now by a night of music and people and booze. Here was the Eliska I hadn't seen yet, the woman who'd cavorted with a Russian mobster, the woman in whom Roger Corbett had found solace for his misery.

"This is it," she announced at the top of the landing. "This is where poor Czech hand model lives in New York City."

The door to her apartment was painted navy blue, and she

fumbled with her keys a moment, then pushed inside. I followed tentatively, waiting to see if anyone else was there.

"Did you even get a drink at that party?" she said.

"No."

She locked the door behind me, her gloved hands turning the dead bolt. I could smell her perfume. "You want one?"

"Sure."

Her apartment was very small, more or less two rooms plus a bathroom. The galley kitchen was separated from the living area by a plain wooden table, and I sat down in one of its two chairs. Eliska took a bottle off the top of the refrigerator and found some glasses.

"Roger's apartment was exactly same," she said. "Just below me. Sometimes last summer he came up by the fire escape." She pointed at the window. Her shoes were lined up neatly beneath it: pumps, flats, boots, running shoes, sandals, strappy heels.

So I was in a space identical to the one Roger had lived in; quite a comedown from his $4 million house on Cove Road in the Orienta section of Mamaroneck, with the sweetly lapping waters of Long Island Sound on one side and a golf course on the other.

"I came to the party looking for you," I confessed.

"Yes, of course I know that," Eliska said, putting down two glasses. "I am not complete idiot, you know."

"The bartender at the Blue Curtain Lounge told me you were headed there."

She nodded. "He doesn't like me, I think."

"I heard you at the party saying you're leaving the United States?"

"I might be."

"Why?"

She sat down, sipped from her glass. Something about holding a drink while wearing black gloves seemed ominous. "Oh, I'm sick of it here. I mean, look at this apartment."

I didn't quite believe her.

"I keep thinking you knew Roger," she said pensively. "It's funny. I mean, strange."

"You miss him?"

She drank. "I don't know. I cannot tell if I am sad anymore. I didn't ever love him, of course. It was not like that. And to be perfectly honest, I do not think he loved me. I was like entertainment, sort of, not that word, but distraction for him. He was thinking about other things, how to get new job, his children, things like that."

"He had a lot to worry about."

"Yes, his mother, his children, money. We could be honest with each other. He could tell me things, and he knew I was not in his life, that I did not care. I asked him about his wife a lot." Eliska glanced from her glass to me and smiled. "Okay, I admit it, she interest me, you know? She telled Roger she work hard to help him with his business career and she need him to make more money. She says it matter to her more than she realizes. This was shock to Roger. They fought about what is enough money in their life. To me this is funny because I am from Czech village where my father fixes his own shoes with pieces from old car tire. Roger and his wife did not have happy sex life, he told me that. But to be honest this was not surprise to me, really, because Roger was not too good at sexual intercourse. He was a very tired man, I think. Tired out. Did not exercise. He was fifty-one and had started to give up. Men give up. He told me that. No one say it, but it is true thing. He said you can look at these men and see they gave up. Maybe fast, maybe slow, but they gave up. One morning I saw him looking at the gray hairs on his chest in the mirror. He said his knees hurt all the time. I think what he wanted to do most was just be with his children."

Eliska's words hung for a moment in her gloomy little apartment, and it seemed she hadn't decided what more to say. And yet I sensed that, perhaps helped along by the alcohol, she needed to tell someone not what Roger had gone through but what she had endured. And perhaps I wasn't a bad audience, given my interest in him.

"He says his wife is good mother and they do good job with children," Eliska finally continued. "He shows me pictures of them, and this is when, you know, he was saddest. He says that when he lost his last job, his wife got breast implants without discussing it with him. This scared him, because it means she is planning to leave him. She did operation when the children was away at summer camp. And she got some work done on her teeth, too. He says he watched her plan it. He felt sad for her. Sad and mad, too. He says he took too much money out of the house and put it into big Internet deal that lost almost everything. He is caught up in it—what did he say? Yes, 'national mania'—and that if he do it all again then he do exactly opposite of everything he did before. Sometimes he cry a little bit, I am telling you the truth about this."

Eliska stood up and came back to the table with a bottle of

moisturizing lotion, Vaseline, and a box of translucent latex gloves. "He is not jealous of my other lovers before him, and this is, how you say, a welcome relief. We are like two strange people who just wash against each other in New York City. Not like Prague, where everybody know everything. No one knows you in New York. That is good thing and bad thing. People get mixed up in strange ways, especially if they are lonely." She gazed at me. "I admit, I am little bit lonely when I meet Roger. I did not mind that he was gray and too fat. I have had boyfriends who are very slim and muscular, of course, and I do prefer it, but Roger was new kind of thing for me."

She took off her black gloves, wiped her hands with a chamois cloth, then poured a pool of white lotion into the palm of her left hand and began rubbing it into her fingers. "He told me when he went on job interview, he has to try to look like he do not need job because that way maybe he would get offer. He said one time he went down to cellar—is this British word or American? I can't remember—and saw all the old china was gone, and he ask his wife where does it go, and she said she sell it without telling him. I think this a big surprise to him, since it was his mother's china, not hers. He told me his wife's divorce lawyer was woman who only handles rich women who live around New York City. Never the men. He said his wife had plan, and she found new schools for children in San Diego and place to live. Her parents live there, too, and she started to fly out there. He said he paid some money to a private detective—"

"Hicks?" The man Corbett's mother hired and who reluctantly pointed me in Eliska's direction, warning me I didn't know what I was getting myself into. He'd been right, too.

"I do not know name." Eliska rubbed the lotion into her fingers. They looked almost spectral, made of wax or marble. "He was supposed to find out what the wife was doing and followed her to big party in striped tent that had something to do with hospital, and then he followed them to the doctor's house, he have four cars in his driveway. Roger says his children didn't understand why their mother and father were breaking up, and the night they flew away from New York his son cried and cried and fought his mother with his fists. Roger said he did not understand why his own mother was so kind toward his ex-wife, maybe it had to do with the grandchildren, he wasn't sure. Sometimes he thinks he should move out to San Diego to be near children but all of his job connection was here in New York. I ask him did he ever have other girlfriend after his marriage broke up, before me, and he said he lost romantic confidence, this is what he called it, that I was just temporary gift to him, and he does not expect I will stick around. He wasn't, you know, angry about this or anything, just like matter-of-fact. Roger was very realistic man, I think. Every few weeks he flew out to San Diego to see his children for few days, staying in Holiday Inn. This was hard on him, you know, and he calls me sometimes from there on day he has to leave his children, saying it was painful to leave them, they are crying a lot. He says he wasn't allowed to spend the night in same house as his ex-wife, but one time when he was there he went to bathroom and checked pill closet—what do you call it? The medicine closet, I mean—and he saw all the drugs his wife is taking and was surprised, because she tries to live very healthy diet, and she was taking pills for anxiety and depression and sleeping and everything like that. It is too much risk to mix drugs like that. His children were doing good in school, but he suspect school was not as good as one before. His son likes to play sports, and he hoped this make him happy. His little daughter joined a swim club, the dolphins or the minnows or some fishes like that, and this was good."

Now Eliska poured white lotion into the palm of her right hand and began working on that one, all the while continuing to talk, almost in a monotone, as if the ritual of rubbing lotion on her hands was hypnotic and loosened her memory. "He says his wife was very worried about future, but he cannot discuss this with her. He is glad he can still pay for children's school. He thought wife's parents is not so happy about her living with them, even though they have very big house, wife's mother has digestion problem, colitis, and father has little bit dementia, put shoe in microwave and made smoke fill up kitchen. I tried to tell Roger what it is like to grow up in village outside of Prague, but I do not think he understands. In fact I think I understand Roger better than he understands me. But that is usual with men.

"He said sometimes he wonder where his life went wrong, and he wish he could do something over again. He said he loved his father very much but did not know him too well because his father work too hard when Roger is schoolboy. He said his father play around a lot when he is younger, and the only way to find out was to talk to people who knew his father, if he can find them. He talks to some old men here in the city and find out a little bit, I think, plus he talked to some people who work with his father. He even bought an old Manhattan phone book on eBay to see if he can find out where people lived. There was one woman who maybe knew his father, but he couldn't get proof. So I think that my friend Roger was in sort of terrible situation in his life, you know? His mother was sick and needs heart operation. She would never talk to him about his father. She is very, what is the expression, close-mouthed about it. She did not want to discuss many things. Plus, of course, his own divorce. Roger is man who has fallen so far from his old life that he does not have way to know where he is anymore."

Eliska was done with the second hand and now dipped the first hand into the wide jar of Vaseline. "So now you see how much he tell me about his life and how I remember all of it, all this pain. I am not trying to hide anything about him from you. There is no privacy left for him, and I am hoping if I tell you all this, then you will have it and I can forget. I know I am younger than you by a lot, but I think by now I have seen some things, first, you know, growing up in Czech Republic with all these old ghosts from the wars and the Soviet control, and then when I was in Paris and my Russian boyfriend and what happened to him and then Roger."

Now both her hands were slathered with Vaseline, and Eliska picked up one of the translucent latex gloves with her fingertips and pulled it on. The effect was strange; I thought of condoms and doctors making their annual exams. She pulled on the other glove, and somehow the spell was broken. What could be more unnatural than to wear latex gloves as you sleep?

I gulped my drink. *Now*, I thought, *do it now*.

"If you felt so sorry for Roger, then why did you store those boxes in his apartment, if you knew that someone might want them?"

"Because he tells me to do it, it is okay."

"You said before that you *didn't* tell him about them—"

"Maybe I lied about that."

"What else did you lie about?"

"Nothing."

This answer irritated me. Small lies usually protect big lies. "Hey, Eliska, why does Roger's cell phone still work?"

She checked her watch. "I don't know."

"Who's paying the bill? Who needs the cell phone of a dead man?"

"I don't know."

I held up my cell phone, turned it on, and scrolled to Roger's number, the one I'd called once before, getting his recorded greeting. She could see I was about to dial it.

She shrugged. "George, are you going to get the boxes for me?"

I could not tell if the question was only that or something more, a threat, perhaps. Had I been too aggressive with my own questions?

"Or maybe you decided to keep them?" Eliska asked.

"No, not at all," I said. "I've been meaning to tell you this the whole night. You can have all of them tomorrow."

"Really?" Eliska became animated at this prospect, and her hands seemed to acquire a liveliness I had not seen before.

"I can bring them around here for you."

"Good."

"But I still want to know who has Roger's cell phone, and maybe now I'll find out." With that I pressed the call button on my phone.

I waited for the phone to ring, and at that moment Eliska seemed to hear something and looked toward the hallway, where I could hear two sounds: her lock being opened and a phone ringing. A big man came through the door, a key in his hand, followed by two other men. He stopped to grab his phone from his pocket and flicked it open.

"Hallo, yes," he said.

I heard this in both ears.

"Hello?" I said into my phone, momentarily confused. Then I realized I'd called the phone in his hand.

Instinctively I stood up.

"Sit down!" the man commanded.

I looked back at Eliska. She was smoothing the translucent fingers of her latex gloves, unconcerned, it appeared, about anything else.

The largest of the three men had an intelligent and fleshy face, not unlike a young, dark-haired Boris Yeltsin years before he'd realized he would never outmaneuver the KGB. Thick-chested, confident of his essential gravity. He said something to Eliska in what sounded like Russian. She shrugged, stood up, and retreated to her bedroom, shutting the door with a click.

"Mr. Young," Yeltsin said to me. "It is time for discussion. My friend Eliska says you have somethings that belongs to me."

"Like what?" *Play the chump,* I reminded myself.

"Eliska has boyfriend, Mr. Rogers Corbett, and before he is made to be dead, she put those boxes that are belong to me in his apartment to keeps them hide from me. This man did not know nothing ever in his life about boxes. And then he get hit by truck and wife take everythings to put in storage. Right?"

"Perfectly correct," I said.

"Eliska says you have the special way to get into storage building."

I nodded, glad I'd never specified to her which facility Roger Corbett's wife had chosen. "I do. And as I just told her, I'm happy to get these boxes for you."

My eagerness to comply made him more distrustful.

"No, you will not get boxes. You will give us location of place that is storage building and the special key, of course."

"It'd do no good." I explained about the list of authorized names kept by the storage facility as well as the security cameras.

He was silent, seeming unimpressed by my explanation. I noticed he had a black spot on his thumbnail where it had been mashed.

The smart thing to do was to keep my mouth shut. But I didn't. "You know," I said, "I was wondering why you have Corbett's cell phone. Especially since he had it with him the night he died."

Yeltsin shrugged. "This is not original phone. Eliska know

his—" He called something to her in Russian, which she answered from her bedroom. "Yes, it is password I mean, she know this and get replacement. I just borrow it from her."

A weak explanation. Finally it dawned on me that if the men wanted to find out what had happened to the rhodium trinkets, then they might have wanted to know who Roger Corbett had been calling before his death. Without the actual phone he'd carried, and its memory, they'd have to request duplicate bills, in that way discovering the numbers of everyone whom he'd called.

"Anyway," I said, "I'll be glad to get the boxes for you."

Yeltsin glared at me. My genius chumpiness wasn't cutting it.

"I show you something," Yeltsin said. "Please you look."

He pulled yet another phone out and pushed a few buttons. He turned the phone around and extended it to me, showing a photo of a young woman standing next to a van with several other girls.

"You see next."

He pushed a button, then showed me a new photo: my daughter, Rachel. Loading up the day before with her volleyball team's mountain-climbing trip in Estes Park, Colorado.

I grabbed the phone—as if Rachel were imprisoned inside it.

I felt a hand rest heavily on my neck. When the hand loosened, I slumped into my seat, the two younger men just behind me now. It didn't matter that I was a lawyer, that I still knew people in the Queens, Manhattan, and Brooklyn DA's offices. I felt a sick panic that they'd done something to Rachel, that it was too late.

But dark-haired Yeltsin was way ahead of me.

"Call her."

I pulled out my phone, saw five missed calls from my wife. I flicked to Rachel's number.

"Wait," he said. "Show me."

I displayed the name on the tiny screen: RACHEL.

"Fine."

I dialed, watching Yeltsin look at me.

"Hello?" came her sleepy voice. "Dad? What time's it there?"

"Hi, sweetie."

"Is everything all right?"

"I just thought I'd see what you're up to."

"Dad, I really need to sleep, okay? We're getting up to hike at, like, four-thirty A.M. or something."

Yeltsin glanced at me and pulled an automatic pistol out of his jacket. I could smell the gun oil in it.

"I'm saying good night."

"Well, okay." I heard confusion in her voice.

"Love you, sweetie. Good night."

I hung up.

"Now I show you this." Yeltsin displayed his phone, which had snatches of video on the screen. "Look close." Mountain sky at night. The motel sign in Estes Park, the university van the girls rode in that day. "We have our man right there."

"I get that," I said.

"He will do what I tell him."

"I told you I'd get the boxes. What's the problem?"

"The problem is too much risk because you know what is in boxes."

"I don't. I mean, I saw Christmas ornaments, something like that."

Yeltsin touched his phone and showed me the screen. There I was, going into Diamond District Assaying and Smelting on Forty-seventh Street.

"Now we know you will lie," Yeltsin said.

He was right. "The storage facility is closed now." It opened at seven A.M., as I remembered. "Also, I need the keys."

"You do not have them?"

"They're in my apartment."

"We make sure."

He checked my mouth, shirt, pants, belt, shoes, socks.

"I suggest I go get the keys and meet you."

"No. We go with you."

They stood next to me as we prepared to leave, being sure I felt their ominous bulk. At that moment Eliska's bedroom door opened a few inches, and she peered out, first at the men, then at me, the latex tips of her gloved fingers just visible, her big dark eyes inches from mine.

It was the last time I'd ever see her.

On the street the men bundled me into a battered van and drove uptown. The time was just 5:00 A.M., two hours to go before the storage facility opened. My daughter would be hiking at 6:00 A.M. her time, 8:00 A.M. in New York. There was something in this, I felt, but what, I wasn't sure. My head hurt from lack of sleep. We drove to the Upper West Side. I wondered if my wife was waiting up for me. We parked across the street from my apartment house.

"Well, aren't you coming with me?" I said.

They looked at one another, uncertain, just as I hoped.

"If you let me go in alone, I could call the police."

"We go with you," said one of the other men.

"No!" bellowed Yeltsin. "Too many cameras, asshole!"

He pointed at the security cameras perched high on the corners of my building. We were stuck. They needed me to go into the building, and they couldn't let me go into the building.

"I want something," I said.

"What?"

"I want Roger Corbett's cell phone bill for the month of February. The bill that covers the day he died, February fifth."

"You do not see we find your daughter?"

"Listen," I told him. "You want the keys to the storage unit, and I want that cell phone bill. When you made me call my daughter from Eliska's apartment, you created a time location for that call. I work in the insurance-fraud business, and we stay very up-to-date on cell phone triangulation technologies. You also alerted my daughter that something was going on. She'll remember that call if something happens to me. And the cops would quickly find Eliska, especially as I've called her before, and then they'd find you." I paused. "So you have to play it my way, guys. Also, my wife works for one of the biggest banks in the world. The security people there are world-class. They have Saudi princes coming and going. She has connections to the NYPD, the Justice Department, lots of people."

Yeltsin grimaced. "I'm listening."

"It's simple. I'll get the boxes for you. But I want that cell phone bill."

The other men watched Yeltsin. "We do it your way," he said.

I got out of the van. I really needed coffee now; there was a lot to think about. I entered my building. The night doorman, James, was surprised to see me.

"I'm coming back out real soon, and I want to borrow a hand truck," I told him. "Can you have it for me?"

"No problem, Mr. Young."

Up I went, into my apartment. My wife was asleep on the couch. I let her sleep, knowing how upset she'd be with me if she woke. I found the keys to the storage unit. Then I called Yeltsin, dialing Roger Corbett's cell number. He answered but said nothing.

"I'm going to eat a little breakfast," I said. "I need some coffee."

He swore at me.

"I'll call you when I'm done."

Eggs and toast. I could feel the coffee zapping up my synapses. Then I called Laura, my assistant. I wanted her to get into the office right away, I said. I'd be making a call to her just after 7:00 A.M. and needed her in place. Of course, she said, surprised.

It was now almost 6:00 A.M. I called the garage two blocks away where our blue Nissan Murano was parked and explained that I'd pay two hundred dollars for someone to bring it to my apartment building right away. This motivated them. "I'm going to come running out of the building, and once I get in, I want the guy to speed away fast as possible."

"This some kinda getaway?"

"Yes." I hung up.

My wife wandered into the kitchen. Under the ceiling lights, she looked like what she was, a middle-aged woman who hadn't slept well. "George, what's going on?"

"I'll take you to dinner tonight and explain."

"We're going to dinner?" Her response reflected how infrequently I took her out.

"Yes. Go get another hour of sleep."

She squinted at me, then wandered off to the bedroom.

I gathered up the various sets of keys, then took the elevator downstairs. My car was outside. I took the hand truck from James, then called Yeltsin.

"Yes?"

"I'll be out in ten minutes."

"Or else we come get you, we decide."

"You have that cell phone bill yet?"

"We work on this."

"Ten minutes. You're going to need a fax machine, too."

Now I ran directly out to my car and popped open the back, threw in the hand truck, then jumped into the front passenger seat.

"Go!" I hollered.

The attendant pulled out like he'd seen too many *Dukes of Hazzard* episodes. He turned the corner at Ninetieth Street. I told him to get out, which he was happy to do, then hopped into the driver's seat and made my next right onto Broadway, going south.

Now my phone rang. "Good trick," said Yeltsin.

"I'll call soon," I said. "Make sure you have that bill and a fax machine."

They weren't following me. I nosed toward Lower Manhattan. At 7:00 A.M., I pulled up to the storage facility, and soon I was inside, pushing the hand truck across the cool floor. Then I opened the unit where Roger Corbett's last effects lay in the separate piles I'd previously made. I found the five boxes of rhodium trinkets and stacked them onto the hand truck. They weighed perhaps thirty pounds each, and without bothering to do the math, I knew that each box contained rhodium worth almost a million dollars, which when smelted down, would enter the global market at the spot price and reappear as specialized electronic equipment or, more likely, dispersed in minute amounts over an enormous number of catalytic converters. I was about to lock the door when I thought of something. I stepped back in and found the 1975 Manhattan white pages that Roger Corbett had purchased on eBay shortly before he died. Then I locked the door and hurried to my car. I set the boxes in the back and the phone book and hand truck on the second seat.

The time was 7:14 A.M. I phoned my daughter.

"Daddy?"

"Where are you?"

"We're on our hike up. I'm surprised the phone works here."

"Where, exactly, are you?"

"We're like a half mile up the mountain."

"Just you and your volleyball team?"

"We have a couple of guys who are going to teach us."

"Big, tough, rock-climbing guys?"

She giggled. "Well, yeah."

"If you look down the mountain, can you see anybody?"

"No."

"Good. I'll call you tonight."

I sat thinking. If I handed Yeltsin the boxes of rhodium ornaments, then I no longer had a bargaining position. But if I was physically close enough to be handed the phone bill, they could take the boxes without giving me the bill. This was why I'd called Laura and told her to go into the office.

My next call was to Yeltsin.

"Where are you?" he demanded.

"Downtown."

"We have your daughter now."

I swore at him savagely. "I just spoke with her. She's with her group on a mountain path. She's safe there for many, many hours to come. Your guy is nowhere near them. But guess what?"

"What?" Yeltsin said, voice miserable.

"You have the cell phone bill?"

"I do not, but someone else does."

I gave him a number. "Have it faxed there, now."

I waited a few minutes, then called Laura. She confirmed that a fax of one page of a Verizon phone bill had just arrived. "Some of it is blacked out."

"Is there an outgoing call on February fifth at about one-thirty A.M.?"

"Yes. That's the last one not blacked out."

She read me the number, and I scribbled it down. A New York City number.

"When's the date of the next call?"

"Five days later. All the rest of the numbers are blacked out."

"And prior to that all the numbers are legible?"

"Yes."

This reflected their precise knowledge as to when Roger's calls ended and theirs began. "Tell me the billing account's phone number."

She did. Yes, Roger Corbett's cell number—matched digit for digit.

I dialed Yeltsin. We worked out directions. They were lurking in their van on West Thirty-sixth between Eighth Avenue and Seventh, so I shot uptown, passed them, then turned south on Seventh.

"Pull next to me, on my left," I hollered into the phone.

Which they did, just outside Macy's. I could see one of the men looking at me. Yeltsin was driving.

"I'm going to catch this next red light at Thirty-third Street. I'll open the car, and you come get the stuff."

Before Yeltsin had time to protest, the traffic stopped. I popped the liftgate, which started dinging automatically. The men weren't ready.

"Go!" I screamed into the phone.

Two guys piled out of the van, grabbed two boxes each, and slung them awkwardly into the open side door.

The light changed. "Hurry!"

The taxis honked furiously. Headed downtown at this hour, they were carrying Wall Street guys eager to get into their offices and jump into the global market frenzy. I started to inch along. One of the men huffed behind my car and grabbed the last box. I pushed the button and closed my liftgate, then glanced at the battered van. The men and the boxes were inside,

the side door sliding shut. The taxis behind us were really lay-
ing on the horns. I let the van push forward to my left, then
gunned it to my right, sped two blocks, turned on Thirty-first
Street, and scuttled west, free.

The phone rang. "We never see you again," Yeltsin screamed,
"but if you make trouble, we make trouble. We know where you
work, where you live, where you buy your wine, where daughter go to school, where wife get her bad hair fixed up, where
your dead mother is buried. If you go to police, we tell them we
pay you money to steal boxes for us. Then we will—"

I hung up. He'd made his point.

I finally pulled over in the parking area of Chelsea Piers,
feeling exhausted. It'd been a long night and a short, furious
morning.

And now I looked at the number Laura had read to me, the ten
digits that Roger Corbett himself had called shortly before his
death.

I dialed, a little fearfully.

"Hello?"

The voice of an old woman, somehow familiar to me.

"Mrs. Corbett?" I guessed.

"No, no, I'm afraid you're mistaken."

"Your voice is familiar."

"I'm afraid I—"

"Anna?" I blurted, recognizing the voice of Anna Hewes.
"Anna, it's George Young."

She didn't answer right away. But her hesitation was answer

enough. "I was wondering when you'd call," she said. "Though I hoped you wouldn't—for your sake."

"My sake?"

No response came.

"You were waiting for my call?"

Again, she didn't answer. How mind-boggling that the object of my quest worked in my own firm. Moreover, what could Anna possibly know? Why her? But I doubted she was going to tell me on the phone. It'd have to wait until I got into my office.

"Why'd Roger Corbett contact you?" I demanded, hearing the frustration in my own voice.

"This isn't a conversation I want to have, George," she warned. "You've sought me out, not the other way around."

"Just like Roger sought you out?" I snapped.

"Yes," she answered quietly, "yes, very much like that."

eleven

A LIFE OF LETTERS

Anna was waiting for me in my office, sitting in the chair that faced my desk, her knees pressed together. She was dressed well as always, hair and makeup perfect. I nodded silently, then closed the door.

"How long have you worked here, Anna?" I asked.

"Mr. Corbett hired me when I was twenty-six," she said. "So that would be almost fifty years."

Amazing to work for one firm that long. "Never worked anywhere else?"

Anna shook her head. "I know I'm not valuable anymore. I

was at my best in my fifties, then started to get arthritis in my hands."

"Never married?"

"Briefly. It was no good."

"You worked for Old Man Corbett how long?"

"I was hired to be in the secretary pool, but he took a shine to me, and they made me the second girl and then the first. So for him it was about forty-four years in all."

"So you knew Mrs. Corbett and the family?"

"Oh, quite well."

"And Roger Corbett?"

"Of course. Sent me Christmas cards every year."

"His mother asked me to look into his death."

Anna nodded. "She wanted someone. I suggested you."

"Why me?"

"You were the logical person."

This made no sense to me. I held up the copy of Roger's cell phone bill with her number on it. "He was sitting alone in a bar just minutes before that garbage truck hit him. He made a late call, wrote something on a napkin, then walked out. He wasn't watching where he was going, and if you look at the video of the accident, he seems to be rechecking that information. I think whatever he was told in that call was what he was looking at, and the fact is this last call was to you."

Anna sat there, composed, her old eyes far beyond me. "Yes, Roger's last call was to me. It was late here. I was in Alaska with my sister on a cruise. He'd called earlier, and I'd left a message that he could call when we got back from dinner, forgetting the time difference. Roger stayed up. He wanted to ask me the name of someone."

I was about to ask who, but the look on her face stopped me; she blinked and yet held my gaze. I sensed she felt that her actions had been honorable and that I must understand this, no matter what she told me.

"You know why I'm still employed by this firm?" Anna asked.

The question surprised me. "I assume it's because you were a loyal employee all these years."

"And no one has the heart to force me to retire?" Anna shook her head. "Come on, George, you can do better than that."

When I didn't respond, she said, "This firm generates more than a million documents a year."

"All digitized."

"Yes. But the firm did not digitize fully until about 1980 or so. Prior to that it was all paper. We decided not to back-digitize."

"And so you know what's on that old paper?" I said.

"I've seen most of it. But more important, I know the filing system for the remaining paper records. Some of them are still relevant today. Not many, but a few."

"They're all in storage somewhere."

"Secaucus, New Jersey."

"This has to do with Roger calling you the night he died?"

"Yes."

"So . . . ?"

Anna was controlling the conversation now. "George, I could tell you, but I'd rather show you."

"We're going to Secaucus, New Jersey?"

———————

I had Laura call us a car. Soon we were outside, waiting for one of those big black SUVs that American automakers should've stopped making fifteen years ago when they still had a chance against the Japanese. But hey, they're comfortable. The car came, and we settled in.

"You never knew Mr. Corbett well," Anna began. "Only when he was much older, after his health declined."

"He was in his fifties when I met him."

"He was a magnetic figure. He worked hard all those years. When I first started, he had to travel quite a bit. The firm did a fair amount of business involving rolling-stock claims. Trainloads of corn syrup crashing, that kind of thing. So Mr. Corbett was always flying to places like Cleveland or Milwaukee. We couldn't always get the local counsel we wanted, or it was just cheaper to deal directly with the claimant's lawyers. I went with him a few times, but mostly I stayed in the office. Mr. Corbett was married to Diana already and had two sons, Roger being the younger."

Our car had reached the Lincoln Tunnel.

"Anyway, Mr. Corbett began a trial out in Milwaukee that spring. We weren't expected to win. I think it revolved around a trainload of hogs that had gone over. They couldn't get them out of the cars for two days, and it was cold, and most of them died. Thousands of hogs. But the hog producer had once been arrested for causing a derailment. So maybe this was actually fraud. Mr. Corbett didn't really need to be there, but he wanted to be, so I rented him a hotel room for two weeks."

"What year was this?"

Anna glanced at me. "Oh, about 1960. Maybe the next year."

My mother was living in Milwaukee then. An idea crouched at the edge of my thoughts, but I didn't say anything.

"He had a fine time in Milwaukee, and I think he won the case. Anyway, when he came back, he seemed distracted."

The car had pulled up to an enormous warehouse.

"The next part is inside this building," Anna said.

Soon we stood in a well-lighted room as long as a football field; it was separated into caged areas, each area holding high metal shelving stacked with uniform boxes. Anna knew right where to go. She unlocked the cage marked with our firm's name, proceeded to a shelf, found a box marked CORBETT/ PRIVATE, dug through it, then pulled out a yellowed folder and handed it me.

"Most of these are signed by me, but he dictated them. A few I wrote myself. You can have this file, George. I think it rightfully belongs to you."

I don't remember the ride back to the city, or even going home that day, because I was reading the letters. There were at least a hundred, the oldest typewritten carbon copies, the later ones Xerox copies. A sampling:

> *Dear Mrs. Young,*
> *Please find enclosed a check for $44.20, for*
> *doctor's visits and ear-infection prescription, as*
> *discussed.*
> *Very truly yours,*
> *Anna Hewes*

I noted the letter was addressed to a post-office box at Grand Central; this would've been only a few blocks from where my mother worked back then, after moving from Milwaukee to New York with me, age two, and quickly marrying Peter Young.

> *Dear Mrs. Young,*
> *Please find enclosed a check for $650 made out to*
> *the kindergarten directly.*
> *Very truly yours,*
> *Anna Hewes*

> *Dear Mrs. Young,*
> *Please find enclosed a check for $189, made out to*
> *the summer day camp directly.*
> *Very truly yours,*
> *Anna Hewes*

> *Dear Mrs. Young,*
> *We are in receipt of a xerographic copy of the*
> *report card that you sent us. All A-minuses and*
> *B-pluses, except for Music Class. Not a bad*
> *record! Please find enclosed a check for $3,025 to*
> *cover next fall's tuition. Also, I will be in touch*
> *shortly about the upcoming orthodontist fees.*
> *Very truly yours,*
> *Anna Hewes*

Clipped to each letter was a copy of the check and the internal paperwork. The cost code was tagged "Deb/PS," which, I knew, was short for debit against partner's share. This meant that the cost of my education, camps, braces, and so on all came out of Wilson Corbett's annual partner's bonus, not his paycheck. This was an elegant way to pay my expenses; the money that went to my mother never arrived in his personal finances and therefore was not missed.

> *Dear Mrs. Young,*
> *It has come to our attention that there is a*
> *summer mailroom job available at the Coopers &*
> *Lybrand national headquarters on Sixth Avenue.*
> *The job is not overly stimulating but pays $4.10 an*
> *hour, which is a very good wage indeed for a*
> *high-school student. Please contact Mrs. Penny*
> *McManus in their Human Resources office if this*
> *opportunity is of interest.*
> *Very truly yours,*
> *Anna Hewes*

So that's how I got that job. My mother told me to go have an interview, and I arrived in great nervousness with three copies of my carefully typed résumé. I was directed from the reception area to a mailroom, where I confronted a stooped old man named Joe. He had a nearly emaciated body but for thick fore-arms and meaty hands, and he smoked constantly. He told me he'd been a post-office employee for thirty-two years. I handed him my useless résumé with grave formality, and he said, "Lift that there sack, bud." He pointed to a very full mailbag. "Put it on that sorting table." He squinted in ergonomic analysis while

I did this. "Okay, be here tomorrow, eight in the morning. Wear a white shirt and tie every day. Get a haircut, too."

I arrived at 8:00 A.M. in my stiff white shirt and Woolworth clip-on tie, sorted through the ten or twelve bags of mail that arrived at 8:15 sharp, classifying them by floor and then by office number. There were three of us, and Joe taught us to order the mail in such a way that we could push our mail carts efficiently through the hallways and be done by noon. Then it was time for lunch, grabbed from a hot-dog cart at the corner of Fiftieth and Sixth Avenue, which the three of us ate outside, watching the women go by and talking baseball. Munson, Piniella, Randolph, Hunter. The Yankees were good that year, won ninety-seven games. The next mail delivery arrived at 12:30, and we were back inside by 12:40, again sorting and making our deliveries by 3:30. We were done at 5:00 P.M., and usually I walked home, ate dinner, then went to see a movie. I did this for two summers and saved my paychecks.

> *Dear Mrs. Young,*
> *We were concerned to hear of a recent arrest for marijuana possession that occurred in Washington Square Park. Through our good friends in the Manhattan District Attorney's Office, we were able to have this charge dropped. Although we understand that not all of the young men involved were guilty of the infraction, let us be reminded that an arrest record is very difficult to overcome and can damage a young person's future in great disproportion to the actual offense involved. It is*

therefore essential that young people of promise be
scrupulous about with whom they associate.
Very truly yours,
Anna Hewes

I can still see the lanky black guy whispering, "Buds, buds," under the trees of Washington Square Park to me and my three friends as we walked by, and although I was too chicken to puff on the joint one of my friends bought, I didn't mind standing with them and trying to look cool as we watched a Bob Dylan impostor serenade the crowd gathered around the fountain. A cop nailed us within a few minutes. I called my mother at her office, and a few hours later I was let go, thinking I'd been released because I was actually innocent of any offense. I'd never given it much thought again, until now.

Dear Mrs. Young,
It has come to our attention that the miracles of
miniaturized computing allow for the use of new
"personal computers" that may be placed on a
desk and used instead of electric typewriters,
allowing for greater ease of correction of written
documents, including student compositions. We
are told IBM makes an excellent model, and we
are pleased to provide one. You may expect
delivery to your apartment early next week, in
time for the second semester, and we would be
quite pleased to receive a report of its utility.
Sincerely,
Anna Hewes

Dear Mrs. Young,
We were gratified by the recent news. Fordham
University has a very fine law school, and we
suggest you contact Mr. Seymour Fisher, who is
known to rent rooms to law-school students there.
If this is agreeable, you may direct Mr. Fisher to
our attention, and we will arrange matters
directly.
Sincerely,
Anna Hewes

There followed a series of monthly checks for my law-school room rental. My mother had told me she had paid for my room with a small inheritance from her second cousin, whose name I didn't know, and I'd never thought twice about it, having no reason to suspect otherwise. Then:

Dear Mr. Segal,
We understand that you are in the midst of
hiring new ADAs for the Queens District Attor-
ney's Office. No doubt the candidates for these
coveted positions are well qualified. We would
take it as a great favor if you would look most
carefully at the qualifications of one George
Young, who is known to us and who we think is
particularly talented.
Please, however, do not mention our aware-
ness to him, as it is through a personal connec-
tion, and we assume he would much prefer to be

judged solely on his accomplishments and
qualifications.
Very truly yours,
Anna Hewes

He'd been helping me every step of the way. A sickening feeling, that, because it meant that my accomplishments, however modest, were not mine alone. And the best proof of that was the last letter in the file, the only one I'd ever seen before, though I'd long since lost the original:

> *Dear George Young,*
> *It has come to our attention that your tenure in the Queens District Attorney's Office may not have proven to be sufficiently satisfying. If you are interested in pursuing other opportunities, we would take it as a great favor if you would consider contacting this office. We are a small, highly specialized practice and offer a competitive salary, excellent benefits, a relatively informal atmosphere, and the ample possibility for interesting work and professional advancement.*
> *Very truly yours,*
> *Anna Hewes*

That night I took the file home and showed it to my wife. She'd heard the distress in my voice when I called from the office and had pulled together a great dinner, poached salmon and polenta, which we ate out on our terrace.

"You seem pretty weirded out," Carol said at last.

"He was my father. I worked with him and didn't know it."

She sat watching me.

"I talked to him, listened to him, worked hard for him, and definitely felt some affection for him. But I never knew. And he knew I didn't know. That alone is strange and sad."

"How come your mother never told you?"

"I've got to drink another bottle of wine before I get to that."

"So in that last call, Roger asked Anna if he had a half brother?"

I poked at my food. "I think that guy up in Floral Park told him."

"Anna gave Roger your name? That was what he was . . . ?"

Yes. I closed my eyes; she didn't complete the sentence. I remembered the surveillance video. Yes, my half brother, reading the slip of paper with my name on it. I saw again the truck hitting him, the paper flying from his hand, disappearing forever.

"You going to tell his mother?" Carol asked softly now. "I mean, you did find out what she wanted to know."

Would I? The revelation that my biological father was Wilson Corbett, not the faceless young man who died in Vietnam, as I'd been told by my mother, tripped one question after another. So while, yes, I was perhaps willing to satisfy Mrs. Corbett's curiosity, she was certainly going to satisfy mine, given that my understanding of my origins had just been torn from me as quickly as the paper with my name on it had been taken from Roger Corbett in the moment of his death.

twelve

THE NAME OF A MAN

Each spring there's a moment when I feel summer coming. The air is heavy, my shirt sticks to my chest. The city suddenly smells different in the heat. Only a second passes, yet time lurches forward. And this was happening again; after discovering that Wilson Corbett was my biological father, that he'd recruited me to join his law firm, and that I'd unknowingly worked alongside him for years, I felt a jolt, a kind of temporal vertigo in which I was both in the moment and already far into the future, looking back at it in disbelief.

When I walked in the door each night, Carol made a point of handing me a glass of wine, and on the weekends she pestered me into going to the movies. It didn't help much; I felt the same way I did after my mother died, walking numbly through weeks of telephone calls and meetings. June ended, July began. I wasn't in a good place. I read and reread the file of Xeroxed and carbon-copied letters that Anna Hewes had handed me, sifting through each for the hidden code that would explain everything, the word that glimmered through the letters' formality, revealing Wilson Corbett's overt affection for me, or even why he never announced himself to me. But the letters showed no such sentiment, and I had to infer his care from the references to his payments for tuition, camp, my first computer. The letters betrayed no bitterness at his obligation, but perhaps he'd been too canny to divulge such feelings in writing. Could he have resented my existence? The fact that he brought me into the firm suggested the answer was no. But I wasn't entirely sure.

There was a lot to think about, and as much as I first intended to do so, I still hadn't contacted Corbett's widow. Nor did I know if she'd undergone the heart surgery she so dreaded.

"You need to call her," Carol said. "It's distracting you."

"Give me three good examples, and I will," I promised.

"Fine. You missed a belt loop this morning getting dressed."

I shook my head. "That's standard middle-aged slippage. Can be dependably extrapolated into early-onset Alzheimer's."

"You are truly awful," my wife said, half meaning it.

"What's example number two?"

"You forgot to make the Cape May reservation."

This was a little more serious. "Only because I knew you wanted to do it. You're oh for two. You have to hit a three-pointer from the top of the key."

Carol stared at me. She really is smarter than I am, and I rely upon that. "You missed Rachel's call and didn't ask about it."

"That's a three-pointer," I admitted.

In July we usually take a long weekend in Cape May, staying in one of the big old hotels next to the beach. I like the town's cheesy Middle Americanness. The kids in flip-flops dragging sandy towels, the saltwater taffy, the miniature golf, the landscape of obesity roasting contentedly on the beach. I fit in just fine. Sure, I've been to the swanky shingle-covered mansions in Bridgehampton and on Martha's Vineyard and Mount Desert Island. Blah, blah, blah. Give me Cape May, and I'm good. Getting a hotel room there is easier than renting a house, because there are just the two of us now, plus you always get a parking spot. It's a ritual for us. The trick is to get onto the Garden State Parkway before 8:00 A.M. on the Saturday. You're on the beach by 1, slathered in sunblock, sleepy from lunch.

"I'm not going unless you call Mrs. Corbett," my wife reminded me a few days later as we sat out on our balcony. "You promised, remember?"

"I need talk therapy."

She got up to water the marigolds. "So talk, because I'll be really mad if we don't go to Cape May this summer."

I had so many questions that I didn't know where to begin. When you boiled it all down, I'd ended up swapping five boxes of a rare, valuable metal that had been smuggled into the United States for a significant revision of my personal biography, for George Young's Life Story, version 2.0. I still hadn't metabolized the weirdness of that exchange. All life is a series of transactions, of course, from the breath we inhale to the breath we exhale, our labor traded for Saudi oil and Lipitor, our faith in civilization offered in exchange for E-Z Pass express lanes on the Garden State Parkway and drinking water unpolluted by terrorists. But most of our transactions are perceptible as such; we know more or less what we're getting for what we give up. My trade had no such clarity and seemed, moreover, to be emblematic of the gigantic and ever fungible empire that is our New York City, where enormous amounts of everything get traded for everything else: your fate for mine, money for fame, time for money, risk for return, information for money, sex for money, power for sex, humor for grief, and love— love for everything.

"Why didn't my mother tell me?" I finally said. "She owed me an explanation."

And yet I thought I knew. It was because I'd already received the love of a father, Peter Young, and if I didn't ever know who my real father was, then it might mean my adopted father, the dad I loved without reservation, would remain undiminished in my eyes. My mother was loyal to Peter Young, honoring his care for me. That left another question, which was why Wilson Corbett didn't tell me himself after Dad and Mom died. After all, we inhabited the same office and spoke to each other a few times a week, even if only in passing. Hadn't he been tempted to just grab me by the shoulders and tell me I was his son? But to do so would again perhaps damage, in memory, my relationship with the parents who raised me. And it might somehow hurt Corbett's two other sons, too. And their mother. So he had chosen to bring me into his law firm, where perhaps he could look over me and derive some quiet satisfaction as a father. Was it painful for him, never to be able to address me as his son? I couldn't imagine myself having been silent in the same circumstance, but we were different men, of course, and if Wilson Corbett had lived larger than I had, he'd also lived with greater dispersal of himself over wider distances. For all I knew he had other situations, other relationships with women or children that he had neither left behind nor fully embraced. Much as I felt a mysterious pain about this, I could not damn him, could not even, oddly enough, wish things had been different.

"What I don't get is how you didn't know someone else besides your parents was paying for school, braces, all that stuff," my wife said, interrupting my thoughts. "You were pretty smart about money, even as a kid."

"We didn't live luxuriously," I said. "I went to private school, but we didn't have a fancy car or anything. I guess I thought they could just barely afford it."

"Could your dad have paid for the things Corbett paid for?"

I didn't know. "Your dad is a very shrewd stock picker," my mother had once told me. "Not that he would ever brag about it." This had seemed plausible, because in his role at the UN he was privy to economic reports about various African countries. I saw them around the house, especially piled next to his favorite reading chair. Such papers often commented on the demand for certain raw materials; maybe he dabbled in those tricky commodities. And yet I don't remember any brokerage statements coming in the mail; I never saw evidence of such wealth when settling his estate. Maybe my mother was covering for him, dropping an idea into my head in case I wondered someday. Moreover, the letters from Anna Hewes on behalf of Wilson Corbett were addressed to my mother at her private P.O. box. Was it possible she didn't tell Dad where the money came from? He ran the family finances; he must have known. That meant the letters were being hidden from me alone. She probably retrieved them at the mailbox, removed the checks, and threw away the letters and envelopes. There was, I thought then, another way to perceive this flow of money: although Dad died of lung cancer in his fifties, he'd paid off the mortgage on the reasonably nice apartment he and my mother bought near the UN; in time she sold it and rented a much cheaper one closer to me, the proceeds of the sale leaving her pretty well situated. But maybe Dad's ability to pay off the apartment was only because Wilson Corbett had paid so many of my expenses. Looked at this way, Corbett's largesse had helped my mother after Dad died as well.

I was on my second or third glass of wine now, and drifted into our bedroom and found the framed photo of my parents that I keep there, taken the summer I was ten, on a lake in New Hampshire. You can see the water, the gunnel of a canoe. My mother, in her early thirties, looks happy. Dad is sunburned, his hair already graying, his sideburns long in the style of the time. He looks happy, too. A man and a woman staring into a camera, all too aware of the years clicking along. If they'd obscured major pieces of information about who I was and how we lived, then it was done with good intentions and not a little discussion between them. With love for me.

But such mental arrangements couldn't have been easy, and so Dad's nightly pot smoking looked different to me now. Maybe he smoked so that he could live with his omissions of fact more easily. The pot smoking probably gave him lung cancer, because he didn't smoke cigarettes, and once the cancer got hold of him, a few well-meant fibs to his adopted son probably didn't bother him much anymore. Or so I hoped. And suddenly I loved him all the more for his silent suffering. So many nested ironies in all of this. Both men—Peter Young, who raised me, and Wilson Corbett, who created me—had made accommodations to each other. I wondered if they'd ever met. It was possible, I supposed.

"So, George, I guess I'll just call," Carol said when I came home the following Thursday night.

"Who?"

"The hotel in Cape May. Tell them we won't be coming. Or maybe you just want to go down there alone and mope around." She held up the phone. "I'm serious, George. I want you to get over this whole thing so we can move on. We've got better things to do than discuss the late Wilson Corbett's pathologies."

"Better things to do?"

"Yes," she answered, "and we're not doing them often enough, either."

I called Mrs. Corbett the next afternoon. Carol took the day off and was packing the car to leave at 6:00 A.M. the following morning. No one answered Mrs. Corbett's phone. *Oh, well,* I thought. On my desk lay the 1975 New York City white pages that Roger had bought on eBay. I flipped it open and looked up my parents, just to see. Yes, there was the listing for Peter and Evelyn Young on East Forty-sixth Street. But it was not marked in any way, a disappointment to me. Did Roger know my mother's name even before he learned mine only a few minutes before he died? Maybe. I tossed the book into my briefcase and called Carol, hoping for a reprieve. "No one answered at Mrs Corbett's," I told her. "So there it is."

"Not good enough. Go up there, knock on the door."

I wasn't concentrating anyway, pushing papers around on my desk to no effect.

"Just barge into her apartment?"

"She barged into your *life*, George."

I couldn't argue with that and told Laura I was leaving early. She gave me a look—not the only one of those looks, either. She knew something was wrong with me those days but not what. I wasn't going to try to explain it to her, either. She'll have her own secrets and revelations to mull over someday.

I still had the fat wad of cash I'd gotten for selling the rhodium. I pulled open my desk drawer, grabbed the cash, and headed for the elevator with my briefcase.

Outside, I walked to St. Patrick's Cathedral. I entered through the massive doors and found the poor box. The cash felt heavy in my hand, and for a moment I thought about what it might buy. I fanned the dollars. *Don't think, George*, I told myself. I separated the wad into two parts and dropped them into the box.

Outside, I walked a block east to catch an uptown cab. The driver read his e-mail as he drove, looking up at the traffic then down at his device.

Too risky.

"Hey!" I called.

"Okay, boss, sorry."

The cab moved quickly. The city is sleepier in the summer; people leave town. We pulled up to Mrs. Corbett's building on Park Avenue, one of the city's grand old piles. I went inside. The air-conditioning hit me. It felt expensive.

"I'm here for Mrs. Corbett," I told the ancient Irish doorman. He called upstairs, then gave me a nod.

I rode up in the elevator and rang Mrs. Corbett's bell. After a moment the door was answered by a nurse.

"She knows you're here," she said with an island accent. "But I don't know how well she'll be able to communicate."

"Did she have her heart operation?"

The nurse looked confused for a moment. "Oh, that's not an option anymore, you understand now."

I was taken through the long living room I'd seen before, but this time the journey continued down a hall that had framed legal documents from Wilson Corbett's career—letters and signed photos from politicians (including Richard Nixon, I saw, before he was elected president), court rulings in his favor, the printed docket sheet from the day he argued before the

Supreme Court—and into a cavernous white bedroom. Mrs. Corbett lay on the bed, an oxygen mask over her face. Around her, on the dressers, stood dozens of photos of her husband and two boys. There was Roger, schoolboy and young tennis player, newly married, a father, and so on. My half brother. One of two.

The nurse bent over and removed the oxygen mask from Mrs. Corbett's face. Her old eyes opened and blinked. She'd been elegant and determined in her agedness the first time I'd seen her; now she just looked ancient and vulnerable.

The nurse addressed Mrs. Corbett. "It's George Young."

She nodded. "I remember," she said weakly.

"We spoke awhile ago," I said.

"I realize I appear debilitated," she replied wearily, "but I remember. I was quite insistent, wasn't I?"

"Yes."

"Well?" she said. "Did you find the answer to my question?"

I had many answers for her, but all of them presupposed that she knew I was her husband's son. What if she didn't? That'd be a shock. She'd die with even less resolution.

"Mrs. Corbett, perhaps you remember I mentioned before that I found out your son had a girlfriend?" I was stalling. "You were not crazy about this."

"No," she said to me now. "I didn't like that."

"But it's true. I spoke at length with her. She's Czech. Younger but worldly and thoughtful. The night he died, he was going to see her. She was quite forgiving of his shortcomings, and I think she was a comfort to him."

Not exactly a lie. It'd even hold up in court, given its general accuracy.

Mrs. Corbett stared at me, dissatisfied. "What else did you find out?"

"What did you want me to find out, Mrs. Corbett? Let's start there."

She sighed. "Mr. Young, my son asked me a few questions about a month before he died. I didn't feel like answering them. They brought up some of my supposed deficiencies as a young wife almost fifty years ago. We had the kind of argument mothers and sons have. I suppose I assumed he'd badger it out of me. Then he stopped asking." She paused to gather her breath. "I wondered if he'd gotten some information, what he'd discovered. Then he died in that horrible way. I told Anna I wished I knew what he knew. She suggested I call you. At first I just wanted to know because I wanted to have it settled in my head. Yes or no. But then I started to hope that Roger *had* discovered the things I didn't want to talk about. He would've liked to know, made it into a good thing. He'd lost so many people, you see—his family, his father—and maybe this would add a person back into his life. It would have made him happy, I know that. I should have answered his questions, it was so utterly stupid of me not to."

"Did it occur to you that Anna might know what Roger had learned?"

Which, of course, was the case, since she'd told him herself.

"She felt you should be involved. Anna and I know each other, Mr. Young, but we're not exactly friends." Mrs. Corbett took a heavy breath. "Things have always been a little complicated between us. She was, I guess I should admit it, very close to my husband. She knew things. She probably felt strangely toward me in those years. She never liked me much."

Which meant that Anna had refused to tell Mrs. Corbett what Roger knew. A little cruel, that.

"Mrs. Corbett," I began tentatively, "I believe Roger called Anna just before he died and received, for the first time, the name of a man who was his half brother."

Mrs. Corbett seemed glad to hear this. "You really believe that?"

"Yes."

"You wouldn't lie to a dying old woman, now, would you?"

"Please, Mrs. Corbett. I'll even show you."

I went over to my briefcase and pulled out the 1975 New York City phone book. With one hand I flipped through the pages and with the other surreptitiously retrieved a pen. "Mrs. Corbett, I have this . . ." I found the page with the listing for Peter and Evelyn Young on East Forty-sixth Street and quickly circled it, keeping the book up so that she could not see what I was doing. "Roger bought this on eBay." I palmed the pen and slipped it into my pocket and stepped back to the bed, hoping the dry old page would quickly suck up the fresh ink. "And I did find this, which, I think, should count as proof for you."

I came around her side, to an intimate proximity, and gently placed the phone book before her old eyes. Then I pointed to the circled listing: the names of my mother, with whom her husband had philandered in early 1960, fathering a son, and of the man who had so lovingly raised that son. How strange to be presenting Mrs. Corbett with my mother's name.

"This old phone book was Roger's?" Mrs. Corbett asked. "He'd found the name of the woman in question, the mother of the boy?"

"Yes. I didn't realize you'd *hoped* he would discover this," I said, stepping back.

"Oh, yes. I'm sure Roger was excited to find this out. He would've contacted this man, I think." Mrs. Corbett's voice was barely a croak. "You said something earlier, what was it, forgiving of shortcomings, you said?"

"Yes."

"We all have to do that," she responded. Her eyes drifted away. What was she remembering? Had she lived a happy life? Did it matter anymore? Now her old eyes came back to mine. "Please come here."

I stepped again to the side of the bed, and Mrs. Corbett lifted up a bony, big-knuckled hand, waiting for me to find it with my own, which I did. When my fingers grasped hers, she squeezed back with surprising strength. Then she looked at me directly. "My husband was proud of you, George. Always." She squeezed my hand again. "Most proud."

Mrs. Corbett released my hand and closed her eyes before I had a chance to ask her any questions. The nurse indicated to me that she needed to replace the oxygen mask. I stepped back. Mrs. Corbett took a restful breath. I waited to see if she would open her eyes, would look at me again now that everything was different, but she did not.

acknowledgments

This short novel was originally commissioned as a fifteen-part weekly serial by Ilena Silverman, an editor at *The New York Times Magazine*. Ilena is skillful beyond compare, and she improved the story in every regard. Also at the *Times*, Aaron Reticker and Bill Ferguson made thoughtful suggestions that refined the text. They were a pleasure to work with. I am also grateful to Gerry Marzorati, the magazine's editor, who approved this project and who offered his thoughtful comments as we approached publication.

At Picador I am deeply indebted to David Rogers, who made many incisive suggestions and helped to comb out the necessary repetitions of a serial and bring the story into a fuller book form. David also suggested the title, for which I'm grateful. I am indebted as well to Frances Coady, Henry Sene Yee, David Logsdon, and Susan M. S. Brown.

My French editor, Françoise Triffaux, at Belfond, offered some keen advice, and I am most appreciative.

At Farrar, Straus and Giroux, Jonathan Galassi and Sarah Crichton generously indulged my desire to bring this story to book form. Thank you, both. At ICM, Kris Dahl continues to provide wise counsel and expert guidance. Thank you, Kris.

Thanks, too, go to our longtime family friend Joan Gould for her advice about the socioeconomic contours of Mamaroneck, New York.

I would also like to acknowledge Susan Moldow and Nan Graham, who were forgiving of the time spent on this project.

And, as ever, my wife, Kathryn.